## Praise for Edgar Award-winning Mark Sadler

"Mark Sadler writes of despair and violence with sizable narrative talents."
— *New York Times*

"Mark Sadler knows both the topside and underside of the New York scene. He writes about both with intelligently controlled ferocity and speed."
— *Ross Macdonald*

"His style has a distinctive resonance all its own."
— *San Francisco Chronicle*

"Sadler knows his onions when it comes to Private Investigators. His Paul Shaw is flesh and blood."
— *Book World*

*Berkley Books by Mark Sadler*

THE FALLING MAN
HERE TO DIE
MIRROR IMAGE
TOUCH OF DEATH

# The Falling Man

# MARK SADLER

BERKLEY BOOKS, NEW YORK

Excerpts from:
"This Land Is Your Land," words and music by Woody Guthrie.
TRO © Copyright 1956 and 1958 Ludlow Music, Inc.
New York, New York. Used by permission.
"Waist Deep in the Big Muddy,"
words and music by Pete Seeger.
TRO © Copyright 1967 Melody Trails, Inc.
New York, New York. Used by permission.

This Berkley Book contains the complete
text of the original hardcover edition.
It has been completely reset in a typeface
designed for easy reading and was printed
from new film.

### THE FALLING MAN

A Berkley Book / published by arrangement with
the author

PRINTING HISTORY
Berkley edition / June 1989

All rights reserved.
Copyright © 1970 by Mark Sadler.
This book may not be reproduced in whole or in part,
by mimeograph or any other means, without permission.
For information address: The Berkley Publishing Group,
200 Madison Avenue, New York, NY 10016.

ISBN: 0-425-11614-X

A BERKLEY BOOK ® TM 757,375
Berkley Books are published by The Berkley Publishing Group,
200 Madison Avenue, New York, NY 10016.
The name "BERKLEY" and the "B" logo
are trademarks belonging to Berkley Publishing Corporation.

PRINTED IN THE UNITED STATES OF AMERICA

10 9 8 7 6 5 4 3 2 1

*To Sheila*

# 1

I WENT TO the office that crisp November evening only because I planned to come in late the next day, Sunday, if at all. I'd been away a week, and the whole way on the jet from Los Angeles I was busy imagining a long morning in bed with Maureen.

The jet touched down in New York just at dusk, and I drove into Manhattan. Maureen had theater tickets, but I had time to drop off the taped report of the case Dick Delaney had just wrapped up in L.A., with some small help from me. Our senior partner, John Thayer, wasn't the kind of man who'd want to wait until Monday to hear the tape.

The corridor outside our office reminded me, as always, of what Egyptian tombs must have been like inside—smooth, silent, windowless, lighted by an invisible source as if by magic. The rows of doors were solid, painted the same pale green as the walls and ceilings, and when they had identification it was in small, reserved, stainless steel letters.

The office next to ours bore the simple legend: *J. BRADLEY GAULT, INVESTMENTS*. Ours announced, with equal reserve: *THAYER, SHAW AND DELANEY—SECURITY AND INVESTIGATIONS*.

"We're businessmen, Paul," John Thayer, our senior partner, never missed a chance to point out. "Brass knuckles and bottles in the drawer are out. We're Madison Avenue, not Tenth Avenue. I'll take front for space every time."

We have two private offices with secretarial niches outside the doors, and a large, impressive reception room. Our furniture is Danish modern, and our receptionists are Finnish blond. It works. Clients who walk in stiff and wary, expecting to meet spittoons and a smell of sweat, relax with relief when they see an office like all the other offices where they have spent their lives.

This night I walked in on darkness, and reached for the light switch. My hand hung in mid-air.

A file drawer banged metallic. In the dark, the door into my private office was half open. Inside my office the beam of a flashlight moved around.

I lowered my suitcase to the floor, and felt a wave of silent appreciation for Thayer's wall-to-wall carpeting. The suitcase made no sound, and neither did I as I reached my door. I stepped inside, and moved fast to the left. I went left because I knew there was cover that way, and because if the intruder heard me enter I wanted to be away from the door.

He heard me.

He turned so suddenly that he hit a chair and sent it over with a crash. In the swinging glow of his flashlight I saw a tall figure, a masked face, and a gun.

The gun exploded even as he was turning.

The bullet hit the wall far to the right of the door. A wild, aimless shot. I found the heavy glass ashtray I knew was on the table where I stood, and threw it hard.

It missed. He overreacted, jumped away, and sprawled over the fallen chair. The gun slid away toward the windows. I dived for him, got a heel in my stomach, flew over his head, and hit the wall gasping. I bounced to the floor and tried for his foot as he scrambled toward the pistol. He got the gun and came up. I kicked his hand. He yelled, the pistol slipped but didn't drop. Before he could raise the gun again I charged with all my one hundred and ninety pounds and hit him solidly in the middle with my shoulder.

The pistol flew from his hand.

He went backwards through the window.

His long scream faded away below.

I stood frozen in an empty office.

Yet, as if time had reversed in slow motion, I saw him hit the window, his feet off the floor, his arms flailing. I saw the glass shatter in bright slivers. I saw his hands clutch wide, then spout blood where the jagged edges of glass tore the frantic hands. I saw his hands miss, his feet thrash, his body twist, and his masked face lean impossibly toward me, and the room, and safety. He was gone.

I was alone with only the echo of his scream.

I walked stiffly to the window. I am afraid of heights. I held tight to the wall that seemed to sway, to be loose and ready to fall. His scream that still rang in my ears was my scream. I leaned slowly out the window.

Seven floors below in the crosstown street people were running through the weak light of the streetlamps. They gathered around a dark shape I could barely see. A patrolman ran up.

I backed away from the window into the center of the office. In the dark I held onto my desk. I wished, now, that there had been a bottle in my desk. But there was no bottle, and nothing else to help me, and the man was gone.

I turned on the light. It broke the shivering unreality of that brief and silent struggle in the darkness.

The office was a mess. He had searched fast and with abandon, and the fight had done the rest. I touched nothing. The police can tell a real fight, and a real search. I went into Thayer's office. It was undisturbed. In my own office again, I used a pencil to pick up the pistol my intruder had dropped. The pencil held it by the trigger-guard. It was a heavy, battered, .38 Special Colt Trooper. I put it on my desk, sat down, lighted a cigarette, and watched my hands shake.

I dialed Thayer's home number. No answer. I called our answering service. They had no message about where Thayer was. I tried his secretary and got no answer. I got up and searched the floor for anything the intruder might have dropped. There was nothing. Police sirens wailed below.

I called the precinct squad room.

"Let me talk to Baxter," I said, and my voice sounded suddenly weak even to me.

"He's on a call."

"This is Paul Shaw," I said. "I'm probably reporting the same call he's on. I knocked a man out my window. You better let Baxter know. I'm going down now."

I had to go down. There was no other way.

# 2

LIEUTENANT MARSH BAXTER, chief of the precinct detective squad, sat in one of my Danish modern chairs.

"No identification," Baxter said. "He was masked, and even his labels are ripped out. Nothing except that gun, and a ring of skeleton keys in his pocket. You're sure you don't know him, Paul?"

"I never saw him before," I said. I was feeling the shock of when I had looked down at the dead man when they took off his mask. "He was just a boy. Good-looking, blond and pink. An amateur, Marsh. When he shot it wasn't at me or anyone, just a scared shot, convulsive. He didn't know what he was doing."

"Maybe that helps, or maybe it stumps us," Baxter said. "What about Thayer? Does he know the guy?"

"I can't reach him," I said, but I wasn't thinking about my partner.

When you kill a man you want to know his name. I learned that as I sat there with Baxter. You want to know who he was and why you had to kill him. It was something I learned then and there. I wanted to know who he had been, and what reasons he had had for making me kill him.

Does that make me sound tough? A cool killer of many men? I'm not. Few men are cool killers. Maybe we all do have violence inside us, maybe it is a dark part of all of us, but we also have a deep resistance to killing: in the so-called civilized countries anyway. We hesitate, most of us, even in the face of attack, or in defense of our children.

I have known a few men who wouldn't hesitate even for a second. A few who were really hard, quick, cold and without a flicker of thought before they struck: in the Vietnam jungles; in the prison camps, theirs and ours; in a few cases I've

# THE FALLING MAN

worked on. But most of us hesitate, which is why we must be trained for war, why we must be made to fear the enemy.

I had killed, except in war, only once before, and that one time had sent me alone into the mountains for a month to think about my life. I had come back to my work, because the good had outweighed the bad, and now I had killed again, and this time I did not know who I had killed or why.

"What are you working on, Paul?" Baxter asked.

"Nothing. I've been in L.A. for a week. Delaney and I closed a case yesterday."

"Anything in that case?"

"Local embezzlement. Delaney picked the man up in Reno."

"Money all gone?"

"I think so. He's going to spend a lot of time in jail for taking not too much money. I hope he spent it all."

"And you can't say what Thayer's working on?"

"Give me some time, Marsh. Let me talk to Thayer."

He took out a cigarette, lighted it. "I don't know, Paul."

"Self-defense, and I don't really know anything."

Baxter smoked. "Self-defense doesn't cut much mustard down at Division, Paul. They kind of feel that private investigators make violence. They figure that if you P.I.'s didn't mess in cases there would be less trouble."

"Just don't lean on me too hard," I said.

"Leaning on people is my job," he said. He picked some tobacco from his teeth. "I know you, Paul. That's okay. I know Thayer, too, and that's not so good."

"John's honest and legal."

"And sharp. You I can trust. Thayer skates thin, works close angles, and maybe likes a buck too much."

"Then lean on Thayer."

He watched me. "Play it easy, Paul. I'll look for Thayer. You want to come down and make your statement?"

"Can it hold for morning? I'm taking my wife to dinner and a show. It's a week, and I'm late already."

Baxter smoked. I was not making life easy for him. He knew me, but I had killed a man. I said I didn't know who or why. Now I was acting like a man with plans who was playing for time. He could be in trouble later. A police detective has to work a lot on judgment, and any man can be a murderer in the right circumstances.

"I can show you the tickets," I said. "Stake me out."

"Okay, Paul. I can work on the gun and the identification. Come in early, and bring everything you or Thayer can give us."

"I will, Marsh."

He pinched out his cigarette and started for the door. He had his hand on the knob when he turned back. In a way, police detectives are actors. They learn tricks of questioning, and after a time they do them by reflex. The sudden question on the way out, after the suspect has relaxed, is standard.

"You said you didn't get in any hits on him?" Baxter said.

"None. It was all wrestling."

"The M.E. says he's got some marks on his face and hands that didn't come from the fall. Bruises, scratches."

"I didn't hit him, and I didn't scratch."

"Yeh," Baxter said. "Tomorrow morning."

I sat for a while after Baxter had gone. I had forgotten to call Maureen, and I was late, but that had happened many times before. I thought about the boy I had killed. He had been just that, a boy. An amateur with an old gun he couldn't use properly, and who panicked. I couldn't tie him to any case I could think of.

Yet he had been searching my office, he had stripped himself of identification like some professional spy, and he had been carrying a professional ring of skeleton keys.

I got my coat and went out.

# 3

THE GIRL STOOD against the building a few feet from where the morgue men were closing the doors on their wagon, and the patrolmen were dispersing the last of the curious. She stood rigid, hands in the pockets of her rough wool cape-coat like a prisoner about to be shot against the wall.

The bizarre cape was in bold red and black stripes, and enfolded her like a tent. Her legs were bare in the cold wind, and her feet were in sandals that looked homemade. Her tanned face was a perfect oval, with small classic features and no make-up. Uncombed, her black hair hung long on her shoulders, and long earrings dangled. She wore an amulet of some kind on a chain around her neck. There were bruises on her face, and cuts on her hands. She seemed totally unaware of the people who stared at her as they passed. Her large, luminous eyes were fixed on the morgue wagon as it drove away.

I had wanted one more look at the boy I had killed, but he was already in the morgue wagon, and I saw the girl instead. I knew at once that this girl was important. Call it fate, premonition, an instant of immediate realization, but I knew that the girl was somehow connected to the boy I had killed. I started toward her.

She saw me. Perhaps there was an expression on my face—eagerness, accusation, suspicion—that told her I was a threat. I had to cross the open space where the dead boy had been. Maybe I moved too fast, acted suspiciously. A patrolman stopped me.

"You want something, buddy?"

I had no time to argue. "Baxter. I'm Paul Shaw."

"The guy who pushed him out?"

"That's right."

"Lieutenant's gone back to the squad room. You want a ride?"

"No, it's okay, I'll find him later."

He let me go, but it was too late. The girl was half a block away and walking fast. If I ran I'd scare her more and probably lose her at once in the crowd on Lexington Avenue. I slowed down, tried to make her think I wasn't chasing her after all.

She turned right on Lexington. I resisted the impulse to run when she was out of sight. She could be looking back around the corner. I didn't fool her. When I got to Lexington, her red and black cape flashed a full block away. She had run as soon as she was out of sight.

I ran, but by the next corner I had lost her in the crowd. There were fifty buildings she could have ducked into, two cross streets, and taxis streaming down the avenue with green lights all the way on the staggered system.

# 4

MY WIFE IS a success. We live in an expensive penthouse apartment, on expensive Central Park South. I like it. There is a view of the park all the way uptown that I watch on autumn and winter evenings when the lights fill the night and I have a drink in my hand. I like the comfort. I like Maureen.

"You could have called," Maureen said.

She was at the picture window with a martini-on-the-rocks in her hand. She is small, and the green mini-shift she wore showed her body better than the tightest sheath would have. Her body is somehow tighter, slimmer, rounder under a dress that barely touches it. A dark redhead with classic pale Irish features as befits a girl named Maureen O'Hara, who has been, for eight years now, Maureen Shaw. If she had not married me she would have changed her name anyway—she is an actress, and a good one.

"I just killed a man," I said. "A boy. Blond, handsome."

"Paul, no!"

I told her. She listened with the intensity that makes her such a fine actress. Her dark, Spanish eyes were horrified, then determined, and I saw it coming—the constant problem.

"How many more, Paul?" Her voice is low, throaty. In Hollywood they love her voice. "You could do so many things."

"Not many, Maureen."

"You like to kill people? Be killed yourself someday?"

"Most of the time I help people, baby."

"God! I wish I'd never become famous. I wish you had to make a lot of money, had to find better work!"

"I don't. I'm proud of my fine actress, and I like the money. I like the people you work with and I meet."

She sighed, smiled. "It was fun in the old days. Both of us studying, working. The bit parts, the struggle."

"It was fun then, it's fun now, baby. It's us."

She hung around my neck. "It must have been awful. That poor boy. But it wasn't your fault, I know that."

"I hope the police know it," I said.

She backed off, watched me. "So cool? Doesn't it affect you? I'd want to scream."

"It affects me," I said.

"You don't show it. You're a rock, aren't you, Paul? The way you were never affected by failure in the old days the way I was." Her arms were around my neck again, her face up. "My rock. I yell and rage and I have you. My wailing-wall rock."

I don't know what I would have answered. I heard the noise. There are three other penthouses on our floor, and there is often legitimate noise in the corridor. The noise I heard was not legitimate. A soft but heavy sound as if a man had shifted his weight against our door. A metallic click against the door.

I grabbed a poker from the fireplace. Our living room is large, and before I was halfway to the door I heard footsteps going away. I got the door open. The corridor was empty.

Both elevators were in the lobby, but the fire door was open. I heard feet running three floors below. I chased down for six floors before I knew I would not catch him. I ran out into the tenth floor corridor, but the elevators were still in the lobby.

I went back up and had a look at the fire door. It was supposed to open only from the corridor side, and the lobby door opened only from the stairs side, but there were always ways for a smart man. In the apartment Maureen watched me.

"Missed him," I said. "I think he had a contact mike on the door. I wonder what I'm supposed to know?"

"Not a gun this time?" Maureen said. The tone of her voice warned me. "At my door? Some shadow of a man? Maybe you won't be killed. Maybe I will. For what?"

"Easy, honey."

"To prove you're a man? Is that it? We live on my money, so you have to be a man another way. I know that's it!"

"No," I said for the thousandth time, "it's not to prove I'm a man. It's just the work I do. If I was an artist, a poet,

I'd live on your money as happy as a clam. If I had something to give, to say. But I'm not an artist like you, baby, I'm a detective. It's what I do, and I like my work."

She found a cigarette, smoked, and held her arms around herself. She was scared, angry, and she did not understand. It's my work, my excuse for existing, the way acting is her work, her excuse. She didn't understand, and it was something we both had to live with. Different people; married; par for the course.

"You like hunting men, the violence?"

"I think of it more as helping old widow ladies," I said.

She smiled. "God, I missed you all week. I'm glad you killed that boy. Glad it wasn't you. Say you love me."

"I love you."

"Good. Now let's go and eat fast and see a show."

They hurried dinner for us at Le Gourmet, and we made the curtain with five minutes to spare.

It was an all-star revival of O'Casey's *The Silver Tassie*. Ever since my days out at Stanford, when I had wanted to be a playwright and actor, O'Casey has excited me. From the slums and troubles of Ireland he distills truth and humanity without illusion or romance.

So I watched, listened, was excited by the power of O'Casey's words and vision in the darkened theater. But at the far back of my mind the healthy, vigorous hero of the play in the first act became a pink-faced, tall, blond youth without a name. The broken, crippled hero of the later acts became the dead boy lying broken in the street. A boy whose name I did not know, or why he had come to make me kill him.

# 5

MY LONG MORNING with Maureen became a quick cup of coffee, and a kiss while she still slept. Thayer was in the office when I arrived. His gray eyes were severe and annoyed.

"The receptionist quit," he announced. "Some second-grade gumshoe barged in before I arrived, told the stupid girl about your adventure last night, growled that the Lieutenant wanted to see us, and scared her out of what few wits she had."

That, essentially, is the way Thayer talks. He's a small man, eight inches shorter than I am, about five-foot-seven, but stocky. He wears a small mustache and rimless glasses, is as arrogant as a Prussian general, and as cool as ice. At forty-five he's fifteen years older than I am, but he seems much more my senior than that. His hair is thin and gray, he dresses and acts like a judge, and he exudes efficient maturity.

"That makes three in eight months this year, John."

"I'm going to file a complaint of police harassment. Where do I find a new girl on Sunday? I'll have to ask the other girl to fill in for a time, and she hates to work Sundays."

He doesn't hate the police, he disdains them. That doesn't make them love him, but he doesn't care. He knows all the law there is. He sounds like a lawyer because he is a lawyer. He practiced years ago, but he found that he liked the police part of the law better. Since no police force pays the kind of money he needs for his bachelor living, he became a private investigator. He is not strong, but he's ruthless, without nerves. He likes the pursuit, the matching of wits. He is not easy to work with, but we complement each other.

"Don't make any complaint, John," I said. "Baxter's leaning over backwards already. Why don't we hire an old lady with steel nerves and no looks? She might stay around. Anyway, we can wait until tomorrow to find a new one."

"A handsome receptionist is worth twenty-five dollars a day on our fee, and I like the office covered even on Sunday."

"We don't have enough to offer the girls," I said. "No men, jumpy clients, and enemies with guns."

"Leave the office organization to me," he snapped. "Now, what about last night?"

I told him. He pursed his thin lips and polished his glasses as he listened.

"I don't recognize your description of the boy either," he said when I had finished. "It could be connected to any case we've handled in the last five years."

"I've thought about Delaney's jobs out in L.A. None of them looks good for bringing on a search."

"And you don't have an immediate case."

"No. What about yours?"

He readjusted his glasses on his nose, flipped open his desk calendar, and began to study it. He has the memory of an ancient elephant, but he never makes a judgment without studying his written notes. It's the lawyer in him.

"I have three current cases. The McAdams divorce matter, the possible security breach at Stanniger Opinion Surveys, Inc. up in New Park, and runaway little Jane Donahue. I'm putting in too much time on the Donahue girl, there's no money there, but runaways fascinate my bloodhound instinct."

"A runaway girl? You have a picture?"

"Naturally," Thayer said, and produced a studio portrait.

It looked something like the girl on the street—big eyes, oval face, long hair—but it wasn't her. The Donahue girl was younger, with much less character in her petulant juvenile face. Still, a runaway girl had friends.

"What's the story on Miss Donahue?" I asked.

"Father's a minor executive. Good salary, not much else. You know the type—all front and bitten nails. Mother's a neurotic, never happy with what she has. The girl ran with the usual rebellious crowd. Father was outraged, so Janey thumbed her stupid nose and did a rabbit act."

"With a boy, maybe?"

"I expect so. We'll find her in some motel with a thick-muscled and thick-headed bully boy. I've got it farmed out to small-timers and stringers in the sticks. You think your swan-diver could be part of Janey?"

"Maybe," I said. "What about the Stanniger deal?"

"An interesting one. I was up in New Park yesterday. They're a poll-taking outfit run by a professor of business at the college, Max Stanniger. People think that pollsters work mostly on political polls, but it seems they don't. You know what most of their work is?"

"Tell me."

"Consumer surveys," Thayer pronounced. "Who's going to buy what and when and how much, and who's ready to buy almost anything. The general mood of the consumer, and his mood on specific products a company wants to sell to him."

"Why does Stanniger need us?"

"One of their reports looks like it was tampered with. Not taken, but obviously studied by someone, and put back lousy. A crude job. I'd say it was copied. Stanniger doesn't believe me, and doesn't know if it means anything important or not. It's a paid-for private report on a specific product, a line of expensive furniture."

"Stanniger doesn't know if it's important?"

"The material isn't exactly vital. Stanniger doesn't have any security, never thought he needed any. He'd do the same study for anyone, and the fee is peanuts by business standards. He can't imagine who would bother to steal the data."

"What does he imagine?"

"Some curious employee took a peek, and won't admit it for fear of making the boss mad."

"Then why pay us?"

"No one admits peeking; he asked straight out. And one little fact bothers him: he discovered the tampering the first day after the report, and his evaluation, had been completed. He figures it's a coincidence, but he's not sure. The report is supposed to be confidential. Mostly, I think, he hired us because he can't figure any reason. He's uneasy."

"Maybe the company that hired him doesn't want to pay."

"They already paid, in advance, and they get the report in a few days. As soon as Stanniger has it prettied up."

"What do you think, John?"

"Some curious clerk. I'm going through the full routine, though. I've bugged the place. I've got a lab on the physical stuff, I'm checking the local competitors of the company that hired Stanniger, and I'm working on the employees. One of them will admit it soon, but Stanniger's paying. I'll stretch it."

I nodded. "Okay, the McAdams divorce?"

"I thought of that, there's a son about nineteen. But I called and he's home."

"He could have friends, too."

"We can't beat the bushes for everyone."

"What's the story in the McAdams affair?"

"He thinks she's cheating with a young buck, and he wants out. I think he's cheating, too, but he hired us."

"Is the wife cheating?"

"Yes, only I haven't spotted the gentleman yet."

"Maybe that's our man?"

"Maybe, and maybe not. Why don't we let the police make the identification and then worry about it? Anyway, he was in your office, not mine."

"An amateur, John. He didn't know anything about what he was doing, so there's no way of knowing which office he really wanted."

"So let the police find out who he was for us."

"We may not have time," I said, and I told him about the listener at my door. "A contact mike is a professional tool, John, and he acted like a pro. Is it possible McAdams's wife hired someone to get the dirt on him, and us?"

"It's possible. I suppose we better go and find out if Baxter's learned anything. He'll probably want me at the morgue."

"I'll call," I said.

Baxter wanted Thayer at the morgue.

# 6

THE MANHATTAN MORGUE is in the Medical Examiner's Building on the East Side near Bellevue Hospital and the river. Lt. Baxter was waiting for us. He slid open one of the crypt drawers.

"No, I never saw him before," Thayer said.

It was a shock to look again at the boy: young, handsome, vigorous and dead. Naked now, battered and ugly, but the same boy and it was a shock. Overnight, and already my brain was working to forget. We forget the unpleasant quickly. I suppose we have to.

"You're sure, Thayer?" Baxter pressed.

"I said so, Lieutenant. Do you want my statement now?"

"In a minute," Baxter said mildly. He turned to me. He looked at my face. "You said he never laid a hand on you, Paul?"

"No. I took a foot in the stomach, and some bruises, that's all."

"There was skin, blood and hair under his fingernails," Baxter said. "He'd been in another fight. Neither of you can tie him to what you're working on? Not even a hunch?"

"No," Thayer said. "And we don't talk about hunches to the police, Baxter. We're not required to make guesses."

"Okay, let's go sign your statements."

We drove up to the precinct. Deputy Chief Inspector Pondi was there. Pondi looked at us, but he didn't speak to us. He doesn't like Thayer; they tangled once and Pondi lost. Baxter took our statements and we signed them. The Lieutenant leaned back in his desk chair and watched us.

"If you think of anything we could use, come and tell me, right?" he said.

"You don't have anything on him yet, Marsh?" I asked.

"No. He's got no yellow sheet, and we don't make him in the city. We've got the queries out everywhere and Washington. We're tracing the gun, but I've got my doubts. That gun's been around, and I don't see him with a permit."

"Physical evidence?" Thayer said. "Dirt, stains, dust?"

"Plenty, but he could be from anywhere. Unless the lab comes up with some pretty special dirt or dust, we'll have to narrow him down before that helps," Baxter said. "He was a real peculiar boy. Shaw made him out an amateur, yet he stripped like a hired gun. You thought about that?"

"I thought about it," I said.

"He's got a ring of pro keys, but he searches lousy. He's got a good gun, but he doesn't use it good. He's got the advantage in your office, but he panics like a kid. Maybe a boy with a lot on his mind he never had on his mind before. Look at this."

He handed a glossy photograph across the desk. Thayer looked over my shoulder. It was a close-up of a man's wrist near the back of the hand. The hand was gashed as if by glass. On the wrist, faint, was a series of numbers: 2437661.

Thayer said, "A tattoo? Concentration camp?"

"No," Baxter said, "it's written in ink. It was on your boy's wrist. Rubbed off some, but there."

"Telephone?" I asked.

Baxter nodded. "Yeh. Like I said, he was a boy with a lot on his mind. He must have jotted the number down on his wrist, and forgotten it even when he stripped of identification. We checked the number, it looked like the break. Turned out to be Carl's Tavern down in the West Village. Nice place, good food. It's their pay phone number. I showed ten shots of your boy to everyone. They never saw him, they're sure. I believe them. Does Carl's Tavern mean anything to you two?"

"I've had drinks there," I said.

"Nothing," Thayer said. "Is that all, Lieutenant?"

"I guess so, but keep in touch. All the physical evidence in your office said that Shaw's telling the truth: the kid's prints are on the files, and the outside lock was scratched up bad with wrong keys. We'll want Shaw when we find out who the boy is, but so far it looks okay."

I thanked Baxter. He could have made trouble. Outside on

the street it was a sunny November day. Thayer looked at his watch.

"I've got work on the McAdams case before I go back to New Park and Stanniger," he said. "You take over on the Donahue girl. Keep a tight check on the stringers I hired."

"Later," I said.

"Why later?"

"I'm going down to Carl's Tavern."

"Baxter checked that out."

"I've got some ideas Baxter didn't have."

"We've no client, no fee. Wait for the police to find out who he was."

"I have to work my own way, John," I said.

"Very well, I suppose you do. Try to make it quick."

He flagged a taxi, and the cab drove off. He hated to work without money in his hands.

# 7

CARL'S TAVERN WAS a neighborhood bar as well as a restaurant, but since it was Sunday I had to wait until it opened. It was on a quiet street of low brownstones in a good part of the old Village. When the bartender opened the door, I went down the three steps and followed him inside.

"What can I do you for?" he asked me.

"I'm a private detective," I told him. "The police asked you about a man. You didn't know him. But I don't think he came here, I think he called here. You remember any calls?"

"On the pay phone?" The bartender began to laugh so hard he had to hold onto the bar.

"It's that funny?"

"Sorry, but it sure is. This place is a hangout for the one-room kids, the hippies, see? They use it like a club. We get a hundred calls a day on that phone. Nine-out-of-ten a customer answers."

"Maybe a call for a stranger. A man, no kid," I said, thinking of the man who had listened at my door.

"No chance. Who remembers?"

"How about a girl? Average height, good shape, tan face, long black hair, sandals," and I described the rest of the clothes the girl I'd chased on the street had worn.

"Hell, that's Miranda," the bartender said.

"Miranda who?"

"I don't know, just Miranda. She comes in sometimes with Doc Cassie. A real good-looker. She was in last night, all right. I remember that red and black thing."

"Did she get a call?"

"Sure did. Around five-thirty. I'd just come on. Phone rings, and some guy yells it's for Miranda."

"Did you hear anything she said?"

"Nope."

"Who's this Doc?"

"Doc Cassie, a regular. Dinner most every night, and the kids come to talk with her. She sure makes crazy talk."

"Doc Cassie's a woman?"

"You know it. She don't got to go home alone."

"Where do I find her?"

The bartender polished a glass. "How'd your guy die?"

"Fell out a window."

"Yeh, okay, that's what the cops said. I don't figure Doc Cassie got much to hide."

"I'm just trying to identify the man."

"Yeh. You got a license or something?"

I showed him my license. He was only protecting a friend.

"Okay, three buildings down. Number one hundred and twenty-four, top floor."

Number 124 was a neat, four-story brownstone with a small garden in front where flowers would grow in summer. There were two steps down into a vestibule. The mailbox of apartment 4-A was labelled with an engraved card: Cassandra Kingsley.

I rang. After a moment the door buzzed and I went into a dim, well-tended hallway with carpeted stairs going up on the right. My foot was on the first step when I sensed movement in the hallway.

My neck hit an iron bar.

It felt like an iron bar across my throat. Invisible. An iron bar that slashed my throat, swept my feet off the floor, choked. I fell backwards. Gagged. Hung by the throat.

Hung by the neck. Pulled backwards. And not hanging, not an iron bar . . . a cord . . . wire . . . around my throat.

My back against something moving . . . harsh breath.

A man behind me and the cord around my throat, garroting, and I reached clawing at the cord sunk in my neck, for the hands that held the cord, for the ears of the head, for the eyes, twisting to see who . . . what . . . black . . . pumping, pounding black blood in my ears, and . . . who . . . what . . . I saw . . .

. . . a small and gray man who stared into my face with his mouth open. I lunged. My hands ripped. He screamed.

"Hold him! Hold him!"

Hands held me. I kicked, punched.

# THE FALLING MAN 21

"Easy, mister! You had an accident. We found you."

The small gray man saying it. Found me? I gagged, swallowed raw pain. My hands at my throat came away red. Other faces above me now. A ceiling with sprinklers. A half-glass door, and through it the sunlight and the moving street.

"You want a doctor?"

"I don't know," I said, croaked. At least, that's what I tried to say. I don't think I said anything beyond a croak like a sick crow.

I sat up against the wall of the entrance hall. I looked at my watch. There was small blood on the back of my hand. Five minutes, about. As near as I could judge, five minutes had passed between the moment I was twisting to see in the pounding black, and the moment I saw the small and gray man and thought it was the same moment and the small man was my attacker, the garroter.

"Any . . ." I gagged, choked, croaked. "Any of you . . . see him?"

"Who?"

"The man who garroted me."

"No one here when I found you, mister," the small, gray man said. "You was just lying there on the floor. I live in the building."

So. Five minutes, of course. He was gone. I had little doubt who it had been—the listener at my door, the professional. He could have killed me, easily. So he had not wanted to kill me. I looked at myself, unaware of the curious faces still over me, around me, in the hallway. I had been searched. Not too carefully, but enough. Pockets out, wallet on the floor, some unimportant papers scattered. Twice now: a listen, and a search, and another search earlier—the boy. For what?

I stood up, touched my neck tenderly. It was grooved and sore outside, raw and sore inside. The blood was only a cord cut: a tough, narrow cord, probably plastic.

"You okay?" the gray man asked again. He was the self-appointed leader of the curious. After all, he had found me first.

"Thanks," I said. "I'm fine."

I pushed out and hunted up the nearest open drugstore. The pharmacist washed my throat, painted antiseptic, and stuck on a Band-Aid. He didn't like working Sundays, and was surly. I found a delicatessen, and had two cups of hot tea. I felt better, could talk almost normally. I went back to number 124.

# 8

SHE WAS A woman, and I knew it. Tall, she stood in the doorway of 4-A in tight, dark-green slacks; calf-high pale suede boots with the tops turned down to show a shaggy sheepskin lining; a gold Russian peasant shirt, belted and decorated. Her blond hair was shoulder length, streaked, and brushed neat. Slender, supple, cool, and a beauty I felt to my toes, rather than saw.

"Yes?" she said. Her voice was neither deep nor light. A controlled voice, all female and aware of that.

"Can I talk to you, Miss Kingsley? Or is it Mrs.? Maybe, Doctor?"

"Anything but Mrs. will do. You want to talk about what?"

"Miranda."

"Come in."

It was her face that saved her from looking like one of those females you know have chosen their clothes not because they like them but because they are expected to impress. Her face wasn't pretty the way Maureen's face is pretty. It was long, and the mouth was too full for the hollow cheeks. Deep creases radiated from her nose, and from around her eyes. Her eyes were firm, clear and relaxed—alert without being watchful. It was a good face that had worn its way to a kind of confidence.

"Sit down, Mr. . . . ?"

"Paul Shaw. I'm a private detective."

"Is it good work?"

She sat down in one of the sling chairs that dotted the apartment. An ordinary Village apartment: comfortable, arty, a little chaotic, with a lot of the sling chairs and at least six studio couches as if she had many overnight visitors. Her head rested against the riser of the sling chair, and one long green leg was draped over the wing. I sensed that she wasn't thinking at all about how she looked to me, as most women would. She was thinking about how I looked to her.

"How do I check out?" I asked.

"Pleasantly. You're well-made, in decent shape, and not extreme. I like tall men. I think you're a bit uptight, but less than most good citizens."

"What are you a doctor of?"

"Psychology. I was a professor. I still am, part-time."

"And full time?"

Her smile was easy. "A roustabout, Mr. Shaw. Do you need labels? One label per man?"

"It's my job. One major label per man. It usually tells most of a man's story, and cuts down on complications."

"Complications are the blood of life," she said. "What do you want to know about Miranda?"

"I want to find her."

"Why?"

"I killed a man last night. I don't know who he was. I think Miranda does know."

There was only the smallest of reactions in her brown eyes when I said I had killed a man. She was not going to tell me much she didn't want me to know.

I said, "She got a phone call in Carl's Tavern last night. Do you know who called her? What's her last name, by the way?"

She hesitated, and her eyes flickered to my left and at something behind me. She said, "Mills. Miranda Mills."

I looked behind me to where her eyes had glanced. We were not alone. A man sat in another sling chair near a front window. He was sunk deep into the chair, absolutely motionless, and I had missed him. He seemed to be looking out the window and up at the bright November sky: intent, withdrawn.

Cassandra Kingsley said, "His name is Jerry Levine. He knows Miranda. In fact, he's also looking for her. At the moment he doesn't really know we're here. He's meditating."

Levine shifted in the chair almost irritably, as if her voice had disturbed the vibrations of his meditation. He had a thick, drooping mustache, and his brown hair was as long as Cassandra Kingsley's. Despite the thick mustache, and long matted hair, I saw that he was young. He seemed relatively short, his clothes were army work-fatigues and high work-boots, and the same amulet Miranda had worn hung around his thick neck. This time I recognized it—the Egyptian Key of Life symbol.

After the one irritable movement, he gave no more sign of life. But I sensed him there behind me all the time.

"What about that phone call, Miss Kingsley?"

She grimaced. "Call me 'Doc,' Mr. Shaw. I'm used to it, and, somehow, Miss Kingsley doesn't sound right after all. Doc Cassie, the female guru. Ridiculous, in a way, but what isn't ridiculous when you come down to it?"

She stopped speaking and seemed to listen to her own words. "It was just a phone call, Mr. Shaw. I don't know who called her, or why. I know she expected the call, we'd talked about it."

"You talked about it, but don't know who it was?"

She clasped her hands behind her head. "I better explain a few things. Miranda was a student of mine at the University of Oregon before I gave up the academic highway. She stays with me when she comes to the city, many of the kids do. She is one of the young people who have discovered our institutionalization of hypocrisy and found it a shock. You understand that term?"

"No social group applies ideal standards equally to everyone or all the time," I said. "I was in Vietnam."

"Yes," she said. "A church deacon is a sharp businessman. A criminal is encouraged to educate himself in prison and take part in society, but if that self-education makes him criticize us we silence him. We say all men should choose their own rulers, but manipulate millions of foreigners who have no voice in what we do to them."

"How does all that relate to the phone call, Doc?"

She rubbed both hands along her green thighs as if that aided her concentration. I felt that dull ache low in my back. She was a strong woman. When a woman is physically exciting, and you add admiration, the combination is powerful.

"Do you know what the dominant groups in a society really fear, Mr. Shaw? Not people who break the laws, but people who deny the laws. Not those who won't work at all, but those who work for a different life, live by a different morality. Miranda is one of the 'engaged.' She believes that the present morality, the system of material comfort, is designed to make us work against our own freedom. We're prisoners of an outmoded mentality. We're made to think we need what we don't need, and those needs keep us working against our real interests."

"This leads to the phone call?"

"I think it does. Miranda is militant in all she does. Yesterday she was a girl on a mission, you understand?"

"Maybe. What time did she show up?"

"About four P.M. She was keyed up, but a little sad, too. In Carl's she told me that she had to meet a man, it was important. She was determined, even grim, as if it were a duty."

"What does that mean to you?"

"I'm not sure. Miranda is, after all, a young girl. None of us can be all theory, so it could be some personal crisis. But it could also have a connection to her 'community' duty. She didn't speak in specifics, but she was involved."

I thought about Miranda as I had seen her, bizarre and rigid on that street. "What makes them all? The Mirandas?"

"Our money, the time it gives them to see and think. They were taught to think for themselves, Mr. Shaw. There are signs that the powers-that-be are beginning to consider it a mistake, are calling for the kids to be taught not to think, but to believe."

At that moment Jerry Levine came to life. He came up out of his chair and his meditation.

"What made you, mister?" he demanded.

He was short, but with wide shoulders. An impression of gauntness, yet there was meat on his big bones. I had a hunch that most of the meat was muscle. He did not live his life indoors. Long hair and a silky mustache give a man's face an aura of gentleness, perhaps because we associate it with the Bible. Jerry Levine looked more like Wild Bill Hickok to me, and a glint in his eyes made me think that he was about as gentle as Wild Bill.

"The rugged individualist?" he said. "Make a private buck and take care of your own? No handouts, beholden to no man?"

"I suppose so, Levine. In a way."

"The big con game! Every man is beholden to someone. All hollow. Make your pile so you can protect your own nest and live free when you're old. Doesn't work. Money for self-respect. No good. Work for everyone. When you're old everyone takes care of you, honors you."

He spoke in those short, hard phrases—like a man swinging an axe to clear a wilderness.

Doc Cassandra said, "Mr. Shaw's a detective looking for Miranda, Jerry. I said you're looking for her, too."

"What does he want with Miranda?" Levine said.

I told him about Miranda and the dead boy. He listened. There was more than muscle behind the long hair and the thick mustache. I tried to recall if I had had any impression of long hair, or a mustache, when the man had garroted me. I couldn't recall any hair, but I couldn't recall much of anything about that attack.

"You know the dead kid?" I asked.

"I don't," Doc Cassandra said.

"No," Levine said.

"All right," I said, "what did Miranda do after the call?"

"She left at once," Cassandra Kingsley said. "She said she'd be back, but she still hasn't returned."

I looked at Levine. "Any ideas?"

"No."

The "no" was too fast. I didn't believe him. "How long have you known Miranda, Levine?"

"Jerry was at Oregon, too," Doc Cassandra said.

"Where do you live, Levine? And Miranda?"

"Over in New Jersey. Near Princeton."

"You know a girl named Jane Donahue?"

"No."

I turned back to Doc Kingsley. "How did she leave Carl's? Did she have a car?"

"She took a taxi."

"If she comes back, call me."

"If she wants to see you, Mr. Shaw."

"Fair enough," I said, and gave her my card. It wasn't fair enough. I didn't care if Miranda Mills wanted to talk to me or not, I wanted to talk to her. I might have to stake out the place.

When I left, Levine was standing, and Cassandra Kingsley was relaxed in the sling chair. I had a strange feeling I didn't know what they might do, together, after I was gone.

With most women I can sense when something is going to happen between them and a man. Not with her. Her face, with its off-beat, but simple, beauty, couldn't be read. It bothered me.

What bothered me more, was that I realized I didn't want to think of her doing anything with Levine, or with any man.

# 9

AT CARL'S TAVERN I got lucky, and, for the moment, forgot about Cassandra Kingsley. The bartender not only remembered Miranda leaving at about five-forty, but knew the cab she had taken.

"We got a stand out front, three regulars. Plenty of business goes uptown all hours after five o'clock."

There were two taxis at the stand, but neither driver remembered Miranda. The third driver was out on a fare. I asked them to tell him I was in Carl's when he got back. I was hungry, and Carl's has good food. I had scampi and beer, and thought about the morning. I didn't see Cassandra Kingsley or Jerry Levine connected to the McAdams divorce—the McAdamses were rich. On the other hand, my strong-armed shadow with the professional touch sounded a lot like what a rich wife might hire to counterattack a rich husband. Had Mrs. McAdams been playing with a dead boy? A triangle with Miranda?

By my third beer I still had only loose ends. One of the troubles with being part of a busy three-man firm was that we had too many cases at a time. We farmed out much of the detail on routine jobs to small-timers—window-peepers, baggers, credit checkers, door-knob rattlers, researchers, repo men, process servers, and a host of other loners who make a precarious dollar doing dirty work—but had to keep on top of all the cases ourselves, and the unexplained complicated matters.

My cabbie appeared. "You want to know about a girl I took last night?"

He was a small, thin man with the face of an old woman who drank too much beer—round, pale and flabby.

"You took her?"

He stood there silent. I didn't need an announcement. I handed him a ten-dollar bill.

"I took her. Uptown, about five-forty."

"Where?"

"You want me to show you?"

It was more luck than I could have hoped for or usually had. He drove uptown cursing private drivers, truckers, other cabbies and pedestrians with steady impartiality. He came to a stop near the river at the corner of Seventy-ninth Street and Riverside Drive: on the park side of the Drive, away from any buildings.

"You brought her here?" I said.

I looked out at the sunny river park where the leaves were all gone from the trees, and a stiff wind blew from the river.

"This is it," he said. "She went in the park."

"You couldn't have told me that downtown?"

"You said bring. Pay the meter."

It wasn't only the fare he had wanted. He was a man who enjoyed putting something over on his fellow men. I held the fare and a tip.

"She went into the park. Then what?"

He looked at the tip. "She met a guy. It was dark, I didn't see good. They walked off to the river."

I paid him, tip and all. I won't play his kind of petty game. He didn't thank me. When he drove off his sour face was rigidly forward.

I stood on the corner. Some luck.

A dead end. Or was it? I remembered the bruises and scratches on the dead youth, and on Miranda. The girl had met a man here only about a half an hour before the kid had fallen from my window.

I went into the park and began to study the ground. It's a fair-sized park, but I didn't think they could have gone far if it was the boy I had killed that Miranda had met. There is a promenade beside the river that ends near Seventy-ninth Street. If what I had in mind had happened, it would not have happened along the promenade. It hadn't.

The signs, marks, were on the grass and rocks some fifty yards beyond the end of the promenade. A low spot at the edge of the river. It had been dark. The cars on the West Side Highway would have been going too fast, intent on their own destinations. The wide river was usually empty up this far.

Few strollers would have been away from the walks in the dark and the November wind.

The grass was torn up in patches for a radius of about twenty feet by what looked like two different sets of flat heels. One set of heels much larger, dug deeper, than the other. The pattern told its own story: a struggle of two people that had started at the rocks on the edge of the river and moved away from the river.

Near the last of the torn patches I found a single button. A large, red button, obviously from a female garment. It had not been there long. I went back to the rocks. After a time I found a rock about the size of a duck-pin bowling ball that rested where it should not have been. It did not fit where it was. There was a stain on it that looked like blood. I found where it belonged some four feet away at the very edge of the river.

I lighted a cigarette. Two people had struggled; a man and a woman, from the button and the heel marks. One had hit the other with a rock. The battle had been inconclusive: there was no blood on the ground, no sign of any body being moved, no other indications of serious injury.

Just two people in a dark park, and the whole city beyond the park to vanish in.

# 10

WHEN I GOT back to Carl's Tavern I called the office. There was no message from Cassandra Kingsley or Levine. I called Mario Albano, a small-time process server who used a bad limp to get the sympathy that threw his victims off guard.

Mario was a decent stake-out man, and he was usually at home and in need of work. He was at home. I described Miranda Mills to him, and waited in my car until I saw him arrive and take up position to watch number 124.

Thayer was out when I got back to the office. We had a new receptionist, another tall, Scandinavian blond. The marks on my neck had darkened to bruises, and the blond looked a little startled as I passed her. In my office I called Baxter.

"Paul Shaw, Marsh. Anything yet?"

"No. He's not in any criminal file, and Missing Persons doesn't have any report that sounds like him."

"How about the gun?"

"A fizzle. Last owner of record was a bank in Altoona seven years ago. It was stolen in a holdup. It could have been in fifty hands since, and none of them about to tell us."

"No," I said.

"You have anything?"

"Not so far."

I could have told him about Miranda Mills, but not until I knew where she fitted, or didn't fit. I spent the rest of the afternoon calling the stringers on the Donahue girl. I told them all to keep their eyes and ears open for any hint of Miranda Mills, Jerry Levine or Cassandra Kingsley. They were all sure they had leads—they wanted to stay on the payroll—but only one had a lead that sounded real: a girl on a Miami flight, and not alone, two days ago. I told him to go to Miami. Just after five P.M. Thayer came in.

"Got him," Thayer said, and sat down with satisfaction.

"Who?"

"Mrs. McAdams's lover. Young buck, smooth and not poor. He doesn't seem like the marrying type to me, but I suppose that's her problem. We can report and close tomorrow."

"Any sign of my boy in the case?"

"No, and I looked. I also called Donahue and Stanniger. Donahue says the boy sounds like ten his daughter knew. Max Stanniger doesn't recognize the description. How did you do?"

When I described my day he pursed his lips, tented his fingers, and considered.

"It sounds like the Donahue girl, except for that man who attacked you. I wonder if she's in bad company?"

"Mrs. McAdams doesn't have anyone working against us?"

"I would have spotted him by now. I'll check more in New Park tomorrow. There was no sign of forcible entry at Stanniger's, but that office could be entered with a hairpin. You're on the Donahue matter now?"

"Looks like Miami."

"Good. Then I won't keep a hungry lady waiting."

I had the same idea, but Maureen was not home, and the cook served my dinner in front of the television. At nine Maureen called to say she was tied up in a script conference. I got out the beer, and installed myself at the television. There was a drama on, which, except for the acting, was as bland and routine as any standard series.

By midnight Maureen still wasn't home so I went to bed. I was tired, with some delayed reaction to my garroting, and didn't hear Maureen come in until she slipped into bed. I patted her gently. She purred, mumbled, and went to sleep. I didn't. I lighted a cigarette and smoked in the dark. I had an idea.

The dead boy had stripped, so he had been worried about identification. He had not wanted to drop any clue by accident. I was sure he had been a stranger in town. He had made his meeting with Miranda on a park corner. He seemed to have wanted to be unseen and unknown. So he would have holed up. If he'd been in town longer than a day, he'd have been in some cheap, transient hotel near that park. He would have wanted as short a walk as possible—both ways.

# 11

THE HOTEL EMERSON is cheap, transient, and on Eighty-first Street near the river park. The morning was gray and threatened rain, and the Emerson was the fifth hotel I tried.

The clerk blanched at my morgue picture. "It's 401. He's been out two nights. I was about to report him a skip. You a cop? I should have known he wasn't a skip. A nice boy. Clean. Is he all right? An accident?"

The clerk was a man who met being shaken by babbling.

"What was his name, home address?" I asked.

"Don't you know that, either?"

I said, "Either? Someone else was asking for him, about him?"

"Last night, about midnight. I'd just come on. Some kind of out-of-towner. Cowboy hat. We get them here. Vulgar people. He didn't know 401's name, either. He asked about a girl, too. That's when I began to think 401 was a skip, run off with a girl."

"What was the name he gave, the address?"

"Ezra Elliot, fourteen Concord Street, Boston."

The name sounded right. A youth with a college education that had included a semester of modern poetry: Ezra Elliot. He'd probably thought about the name all the way into the city. No John Smith for him.

I called Lt. Baxter. The brass at Detective Division aren't happy when a private investigator even delays information in a homicide. I had killed the boy, and this was as far as I went alone. I stayed right with the clerk until Baxter arrived dripping from the rain that had started.

"How'd you find the place?" he asked me.

I gave him the story of Miranda Mills, and mentioned the man in the cowboy hat who'd been there last night.

"You could have told me sooner, Paul."

"I had nothing definite to bring the girl in until now. It was a hunch, no more."

"Okay. Any ideas about the cowboy?"

"Only that he was looking after the kid was dead. He could know why the kid came to my office. The break, maybe."

"If we ever see him again. Let's go up."

Baxter inspected the outside door of room 401 before he unlocked it. Inside, it was the typical cubicle with one window on an air shaft, a shabby studio couch, and fire-sale furniture. It had been vaguely cleaned by a maid.

"It looks untouched," Baxter said.

"Dust on the bureau."

There was one suitcase with a single change of clothes in it, an extra pair of shoes, and personal effects inside the top bureau drawer. The wastebasket had been emptied, but one torn label from a suit lay in the bottom. The personal effects were a ring of house keys, a chain of car keys, a cigarette lighter monogrammed *J.B.C.*, a pack of cigarettes, and a wallet with a few credit cards in plastic slots.

"Jon B. Calvin," Baxter read. "No *h* in Jon."

So I knew the name of the man I had killed. I should have felt better. I didn't. It was the room—a sad room, almost pitiful. In this cheap room a boy had stripped of all identification like some super-spy who expected capture by evil Soviet agents or the Gestapo. He had taken skeleton keys, mask and gun, and gone out into the night on some vital mission. Too many spy novels, too many movies, and no judgment. A boy driven by fear or need to a desperation he couldn't handle.

"Home address seems to be Kingston, New York," Baxter read. "Parents at the same address. But there're some rent receipts from a place in New Park, New York, too."

There was the connection. New Park: Stanniger Surveys, Inc. I filled Baxter in on what Thayer had told me about that case.

"You figure this Calvin fiddled with that report?"

"It's the connection to us. Maybe he thought we knew more than we do. Or wanted to find out what we did know."

"Okay. I'll report, notify Kingston and New Park, and get to the parents. That about wraps it up."

"We don't know what's behind it, Marsh."

"Maybe we never will. We need crimes to work on, Paul. Calvin did the breaking-and-entering, and he's dead. You're clean as far as I'm concerned. If Kingston or New Park want us to do more, they'll have to come up with evidence."

He meant evidence to show that there was something more to Calvin's death, and my part in it, than there appeared to be, or than I was telling him. It was not a pleasant thought for me. It made me edgy, and I jumped when someone knocked on the door of the room. Baxter opened the door.

The man who stood there wore a wet black slicker, and a broad-brimmed, pearl-gray Stetson soggy with rain. A cowboy hat. The man who had been asking after Jon Calvin last night. I moved toward him by reflex. He might have all the answers to end it. I wanted it to end. He ignored my move toward him.

"Lieutenant Baxter?" he said, drawled. He had a slow voice, with a habit of authority in it.

"That's right," Baxter said.

The man ambled into the room leaving a wet trail. He was tall and thin. Under the slicker he wore a brown suit that showed years of frugal care. Maybe fifty-five, and almost skinny, he looked hard as a whip. He had the craggy face of a rustic church deacon, thick iron-gray hair, and small eyes that took me in at a glance. A lump at his side under the suit had to be a pistol in a side holster.

"Sergeant Sam Norman, Wayne Center Police," he said to Baxter. "Guy on the desk said you was up here. My kid dead?"

I said, "You're after Jon Calvin, Sergeant? What for?"

He gave me a slow stare, and spoke to Baxter. "Not after him, Lieutenant, looking for him. What happened?"

Baxter told him. My hope of quick answers was fading. There is a difference between being after a man, and looking for him. When Baxter got to the part about the fight in my office, Norman looked at me. I couldn't tell whether he was sympathetic, suspicious, or just trying to decide if I was capable of knocking a healthy youth out a seven-story window.

When Baxter finished, Norman lighted a cigarette. "So it was too late before I got started. Eric Calvin's gonna take it bad. You got any ideas what Jon wanted from you, Shaw?"

"Do you?" I said.

"Can't say I do. The boy just went off sudden early Friday without telling no one. His folks figured it was a girl."

"Miranda Mills?"

He seemed to get more respect for me. "That's her. One of those crazy flower kids. There's a camp of them in the hills near New Park. Jon was fooling around up there."

So the long-haired meditator in Cassandra Kingsley's apartment, Jerry Levine, had lied. Miranda Mills lived at the New Park camp, and I had a good hunch Jerry Levine lived there, too. Why had he lied, and why had Dr. Cassandra Kinsley let him lie? She had to know where they lived.

Baxter said, "Then this is unofficial, Sergeant?"

"Yeh. A favor for Mr. MacDougall."

"Who the hell's Mr. MacDougall?" Baxter said. He was getting impatient with the slow village cop.

"Mr. MacDougall lives in Wayne Center," Norman said, unperturbed. "He's Eric Calvin's boss," he went on like a father explaining to a backward child. "We're sort of a suburb of Kingston. Small, you know? Mr. MacDougall carries the weight, right? So when Eric Calvin gets worried about Jon, and tells old MacDougall, I say maybe I can find the kid and talk some sense. A little extra money, right? Eric Calvin put out a lot of scratch to send that boy through college, he wasn't about to see the kid toss away his future on some way-out female. Only I guess he got no future at all now."

Norman's small eyes seemed to be saying that maybe I could have handled Jon Calvin without killing him; that he, Sam Norman, could have. Maybe he could have, and maybe I could have if I had known who I was dealing with in the dark office. But I hadn't known, and there was no going back.

"What company does Eric Calvin work for?" I asked.

"Regent-Crown Furniture. They're in Kingston."

The report that had been tampered with at Stanniger's was for a furniture company.

"Was Jon Calvin connected to Stanniger Surveys, Inc.?"

"You mean that outfit down New Park?" Norman said. "Not that I know. New Park's out of my territory."

Baxter said, "When did you start looking, Sergeant?"

"Last night. I looked around New Park, found his car at the bus terminal. He'd bought a ticket for New York, so I come down."

# THE FALLING MAN　　　　　　　　　37

"He had a car," I said, "but he took the bus?"

"I guess he didn't want to be found easy."

"Last night," Baxter said, "and you didn't come to us?"

"Well now," Norman drawled, "it was private, right? The Calvins figured it was girl trouble. Nothing for the cops, and they wanted it quiet. So I looked around for him, asked for the girl, checked out the hospitals and the bars his old man said he'd talked about sometimes, and then came back up here. If I didn't find him this time, I was gonna get around to the cops."

"How did you find this place? You were here last night," I said.

"That's right, about midnight. Eric Calvin told me Jon lived a couple of months one time around Seventy-second Street. It sounded like he'd been alone on the bus. I figured that when a guy comes to meet a girl in a big city he goes where he knows his way around. I wasted some time on the taxis down at the West Side Terminal. He didn't take one as far as I could find out. So I came up and started working my way through the hotels around here."

"That sounds like a lot of work," I said.

"I'll get paid," Norman said drily. "Anyway, that's what police work is, right? I picked up this place around midnight. He wasn't here, like you know. So I kept looking. Now I got to tell the Calvins. I don't much like that."

"Can you identify the boy?" Baxter asked.

"Yeh, I seen him and his old man around MacDougall's place at company picnics plenty of times. We got a pretty small force up Wayne Center. We get a kind of bonus for policing those picnics, you know?"

"Okay," Baxter said. "Let's go to the morgue."

Norman nodded. "I guess that's part of what I'm getting paid for. I mean, I found him, didn't I?"

# 12

IN THE OFFICE Thayer was closeted with our divorce client, McAdams. Mario Albano had left a message that there was no sign of Miranda Mills yet, and no other action at number 124. I called Max Stanniger in New Park.

"Paul Shaw, Mr. Stanniger. John Thayer's partner."

"Of course. You have something?" Stanniger had a crisp, clipped voice, yet smooth and sincere as if he was accustomed to selling strangers on the telephone.

"Does the name Jon Calvin mean anything to you?"

"No. Calvin? Jon Calvin?"

"That's it."

"Hold on."

I held on. Inside Thayer's office McAdams was shouting, and Thayer was soothing. Max Stanniger came back on the line.

"Shaw? My personnel manager, Mrs. Driscoll, has a Jon Calvin on her part-time list. We hire part-timers in batches when we need them for tabulating results and making telephone interviews. Calvin was one of twenty we took on about a month ago. He's still supposed to be working, but he hasn't shown for a few days."

"Is Regent-Crown the company involved in the tampered report?"

"Yes it is. Is Jon Calvin mixed up in this?"

"Weren't you suspicious when he didn't show?"

"No. At least six of the present part-time group were missing some days this week. They come and go. We only pay for hours worked. I never see them. They're only names on a roster even to Mrs. Driscoll."

"How about Miranda Mills?"

"Hold on again."

This time he was gone only seconds. Mrs. Driscoll must have been standing beside him with her roster. Stanniger said, "Miranda Mills is another of the part-timers, yes. She's been out the same days as Calvin. Are they . . . ?"

"Thayer'll be up later to talk," I said.

"Wait! Shaw?"

I waited. "What is it?"

"I have something for you. I was discussing the whole thing with my staff last evening, and one of my people recalled that Walter Tyrone had contacted him a few weeks ago about doing a poll much like the Regent-Crown survey. Tyrone asked about fees, time involved, how we did it, all that."

"Is that important?"

"Tyrone is president of Hudson Furniture, Inc. They're in Kingston, too. Direct competitors. It's probably nothing, but Tyrone never followed up on the initial inquiry. They usually do follow up, but Tyrone seems to have dropped the matter."

I got the point. "All right, I'll tell Thayer."

I hung up, thought about Hudson Furniture and the obvious, and heard McAdams leave. Thayer came into my office. He was pale.

"Took it bad at first," Thayer said, mopping his face, "but that could have been an act. I hope he doesn't try to kill the man."

"That would be annoying," I said. There are times when Thayer's cool detachment irks me.

"Messy," Thayer agreed. "You were late today?"

I gave him the details of my morning. When he heard about my conversation with Stanniger, he beamed.

"That should wrap up another one then. Calvin's our boy. I'll go up and get the proof. It should be a breeze now."

"Maybe," I said. "Why was Calvin so desperate, John? It's a two-bit affair. About all they'd do is fire him."

"Not if we prove he sold the data. That's criminal. He got it, sold it to Hudson Furniture cut-rate. An employee and a direct competitor. Always look for the obvious."

"Unless it isn't the obvious."

Thayer tented his hands again, and let my accusation lie there between us like a long dead fish. He studied me through those rimless glasses, fingered his mustache.

"You know," he said at last, "there's one thing you still

haven't learned, Paul. Our business isn't to solve crimes, it's to solve clients' problems. Stanniger wants to know who tampered with his report, and, if possible, where the data went. I don't care what the motive was, or what else Calvin may have had on his mind. His reasons don't interest me."

He twisted his mustache. "You've laid out the pieces. Calvin worked unseen, almost, at Stanniger's. His father works at Regent-Crown, is friendly with Angus MacDougall, who happens to be Regent-Crown's executive vice-president. He heard about the survey, had the chance, and took it. Why he did is no concern of ours, unless it helps to prove our case."

"What about the man who jumped me?"

"Calvin wasn't in it alone. Or perhaps that man is working for the buyer of the data. I'll find out."

"How did Calvin know about us? You're not usually spotted so easily on a job."

"Probably MacDougall again. Stanniger told him, of course. MacDougall talked where the boy heard. The boy then panicked."

I had no answer, and Thayer left for New Park before lunch. I worked on the Donahue girl by telephone. I thought about Miranda Mills. Why was she missing even from her friends, if she was? I don't like unanswered questions.

I ate lunch at my desk, and at one o'clock I heard voices in the reception room. One was loud, strident. The other was lower. I heard my name on a rising note from the strident voice. I rested my hand on the Colt Commander in my drawer.

The intercom buzzed. "Mr. Calvin and Mr. MacDougall to see you."

# 13

THE SMALLER OF the two men pushed in first as if he couldn't wait to see my face. A muscle twitched near his right eye. His large hands hung unnaturally loose. His old suit was navy-blue and double-breasted, and he had not stopped to press it. I stood up.

"I'm Paul Shaw, Mr. Calvin. I'm sorry."

My palms sweated, and my right hand hung close to the gun in my drawer. A man must hate another man who killed his son no matter what the cause. Eric Calvin's face twitched, and he stared at me. I saw that there was no real violence in him. Only pain and questions.

"You killed my son?!"

It was as much a question as an accusation. I had killed his son, and no matter how justified, there were always the questions. Did you have to *kill* him? Couldn't you have? . . . Why didn't you? . . . Was there no other? . . . All the hopeless questions I would have asked if it had been my son.

"I'm sorry," I said. What more could I say?

His mouth twisted as if his unsaid words hurt. His eyes fixed on the repaired window, obsessed. He was about fifty, square-faced and rough-featured, with not much gray in his thin brown hair. His blue eyes were red now, and there were deep lines in his face that had come from years of some meticulous work. The nails and creases of his large hands were stained with ground-in grime that was permanent. The story of much of his life was in those hands—workingman's hands.

"Eric knows that, Mr. Shaw. We spoke with Lieutenant Baxter," the second man said. "I'm Angus MacDougall."

MacDougall was a large man who made Eric Calvin seem smaller than he was. Almost a hearty, shaggy bear except for a certain reserved stiffness. At first glance MacDougall looked the younger of the two. He wasn't. He was well-groomed, and well-cared-for, but there was white in his immaculate hair. There was authority in his whole manner, but he didn't seem to push it. His gray suit was good but not extravagant, and everything he wore matched tastefully. His brown eyes were strong and alert, and when he glanced toward Eric Calvin I saw that he had vanity. I caught the faint reflection of contact lenses instead of glasses.

"You accept Baxter's belief in my story?" I said.

Eric Calvin did not look at me. "Yes."

"A sad tragedy," MacDougall said. "We all wish it had ended otherwise, but Eric understands that one cannot always choose the outcome of a struggle. Although that doesn't help much."

"I don't suppose anything would."

"There might be some relief if Eric knew more of why it happened," MacDougall said. "That's why we're here."

"I'll tell you anything I find out."

"Eric wants more than that," MacDougall said.

Eric Calvin sat down in one of my Danish chairs, leaned at me. "I want to know why Jon came here, why he had a gun! I want to know what was behind it. Jon was a fine boy. If he attacked you, someone was behind it all!"

The tautness in his voice stretched thinner, unable to believe that his son had done wrong. It was there in the single word—"if". *If* Jon had attacked me. The "if" would never leave his mind until he had a face and a name to blame, to fix his hate on. Until then he could only blame his son, or himself, and the "if" would never leave his mind.

"Exactly what do you want, Mr. Calvin?"

"To hire you. I want to find out who got Jon into this. He was never in trouble in his life! He was a hard-working boy. I sent him to college, but every summer he worked in the factory with me. He knew what a man had to do. He would have been an officer in the army except for a football injury to his knee. He was a happy boy, eager. He was strong, bright, handsome . . ."

Calvin's voice didn't break, it faded away to a whisper. As if he was talking to his dead son, telling Jon how much he, Eric, had loved him, how good a boy he had been. I remembered the dead face in the street. The dead boy had probably been all his father said. But the masked youth in my office, with his skeleton keys and gun, had been something else.

"I have a client, I'm sorry," I said.

MacDougall said, "Stanniger? That's just why we want to hire you. How do we know Stanniger himself isn't mixed up in all of it?"

"Your company hired Stanniger."

"Not by my choice," MacDougall snapped. "It's no secret what I think of those poll outfits, but that isn't the issue now. Stanniger hired you to find out who tampered with our report, if anyone did, and you won't go any farther than exposing who the tamperer was to Stanniger. We want more than that."

For a moment I almost wondered if MacDougall had been talking to Thayer, and Thayer had forgotten to mention it to me. But I decided that couldn't be. Thayer never forgot anything. MacDougall was just a smart businessman who knew how the world worked.

"We come high, Mr. MacDougall."

"I can pay the bill, Mr. Shaw. Eric is a friend of thirty years. He's been our glue-room foreman for twenty years. Men have responsibilities to each other after that much time. Eric's son is dead. He wants to know why."

"You know we think that Jon tampered with that report, probably stole the data?"

Eric Calvin came out of his silent reverie of communion with his dead son. "No! Jon never stole a dime in his whole life. It was that girl. He got involved with her, I know it. The filthy little bitch!"

"Miranda Mills?" I said.

"Easy, Eric," MacDougall said. "We don't know."

Eric Calvin brushed that aside. He looked at me, not at MacDougall. "That's her, yes. I didn't think that there was anything serious. I knew Jon went to that pig-pen they call a camp sometimes, but he laughed about them. I don't know how she got her hooks into him, or even why. The usual way, I suppose. Jon was a normal man, and those bums have no morals."

"You didn't think there was anything serious, but now you do. Why? Did Jon say anything before he left?"

"No, he was seen with her by people who know me."

MacDougall said, "Me, for one. I saw them in New Park when I went to talk to Stanniger the day before Jon vanished."

"She's missing from that camp," Eric Calvin said. "I went there. She's behind it all, I know it!"

"How did Miranda Mills know the survey existed?" I asked. "She only worked part-time at Stanniger's."

"Jon only worked there part-time," Eric Calvin said.

MacDougall knew what I was getting at. "Let's face it, Eric," he said, "Jon had every chance to learn about the survey. I probably spouted about it fifty times around him."

"Wasn't it confidential, Mr. MacDougall?"

"The results were supposed to be, if you believe Stanniger, but its existence wasn't. It's not very secret, and those polls are a pet peeve of mine. Crutches for management men afraid to trust their own judgment. We didn't build American industry on outside experts and academic consultants."

"Do you think Jon stole the data to sell?"

"I don't know what to think," MacDougall said.

Eric Calvin said, "What was it worth? You said it, Mr. MacDougall, it isn't so secret. A consumer poll. You can read opinion surveys like that in the newspapers. Who the hell would buy the raw data? What it says doesn't matter until you in management decide what to do about the results. Even then, what the hell is it worth?"

"All I can say, Eric," MacDougall said, "is that it looks like someone thought it had value."

"Sure! Those damned hippie bums!"

"We don't know that, Eric," MacDougall said.

"Then let's find out! That's what I want, Shaw."

He was working hard to channel his pain, his despair for a son who would never come home, into something he could deal with. Something that would help him go on living with a dead son, day-in and day-out—hate for someone. He needed a way to forget, to fill his life with something besides a memory. He had to have something to think about in the slow hours.

"I don't see how we can have two clients," I said.

Calvin's big hands clenched. "Don't you want to find out, Shaw? Or maybe you know more than you're telling? You killed my boy, do you just want to forget it?"

"All right, pay my secretary an advance on the way out. She'll tell you how much," I said. "But remember, if there is a conflict, Stanniger is our first client, and I find the truth no matter what. Agreed?"

"Yes," Eric Calvin said. "The truth. That's what I want."

# 14

THROUGH MY OPEN door I watched them leave. I went back to my desk. I sat down and closed the drawer on my pistol. Outside, low, black clouds raced across the city, shredded on the high buildings. I sat and looked out the window where Jon Calvin had fallen with the long, fading scream.

Why had he searched my office? Because he wanted to find out what we knew. Why? Because he had stolen the data on the Regent-Crown survey. But the survey had little value, everyone seemed to agree on that, and who would pay enough for it to make Jon Calvin take the risks? Why had he seemed so desperate? Even if caught all the way, it was still a minor charge.

I went to the window. I held onto the wall. I could feel the pull of the wind as I looked down at the street where Jon Calvin had died. The trouble with real police work is that it doesn't move in a neat circle but in a straight line. Step by step, most of the time, without all the pieces at hand. Not a neat, contained puzzle, but a chaos of lines that too often never met or came to dead, loose ends. You can trail a hundred leads, only to solve the case in an instant when some totally unknown factor appears by chance—something, or someone, never in the case before. Not a matter of thinking, but of walking: dogged, weary walking until you just bump into the answer.

I saw them far below—Eric Calvin and MacDougall. On the street where Jon Calvin had fallen. I recognized the neat, gray topcoat and gray homburg MacDougall had put on in the reception room, and the bright, incongruous mackinaw of Eric Calvin. They were standing across the street from my building, looking in silence toward the spot where Jon Calvin had hit. Like two silent ships on a gray sea hovering in homage over the spot where another ship had sunk from sight forever. For them it was more than a case, an uneasy mystery, it was an impossible rock in their smooth lives.

I saw MacDougall touch Eric Calvin on the arm, gently. The two men began to walk toward Lexington Avenue.

Then I saw the third man.

He came from out of sight on my side of the street, angled across in mid-block through the traffic, and vanished into the shadows of the building opposite. I waited. I could no longer see him, but I sensed him there close to the wall of the opposite building in the dark afternoon. Up the block, MacDougall and Eric Calvin had stopped. When they began to walk again, I saw the movement of the third man as he followed them. He moved close to the buildings, trying to not be seen.

I stepped back from the window. A fast look, no more, but I knew the third man. I knew the broad, muscular build, the army fatigues, the long, silky hair to his shoulders. Jerry Levine. Miranda's "friend" who had not known anything about Jon Calvin, and who had lied about where he and Miranda lived. Following Jon Calvin's father, and Angus MacDougall from Regent-Crown.

After I sat and thought about it for a time, I asked Thayer's secretary to call him in New Park. His motel said he wasn't there. He wasn't with Stanniger, either. No one knew where he was. I went back to work on the Donahue girl, with no luck. I felt like a solitary bird far out at sea looking for a place to land. B five o'clock I was ready to start for New Park myself.

Then Mario Albano called. "Your bird's in the nest."

# 15

A MUDDY VOLKSWAGEN was parked in front of number 124. Mario Albano nodded at the car, and limped away. We'd get his bill, padded, tomorrow morning. I went up.

Dr. Cassandra Kingsley was definitely not a woman who worried much about her clothes. She wore the same clothes she had worn yesterday. The slacks and boots looked just as good.

"So you had us watched?"

"Why'd you lie, Doc?" I said. "You know where they live."

"It was Jerry's decision to make, not mine. Whatever his reasons for not telling you were, I respect them."

"What were his reasons?"

She closed the door behind me, and leaned against it as I stood in the apartment. It was a pose that showed her off: long legs crossed at the ankles in the boots, breasts high, her finely etched face quiet. I understood part of her attraction. When not in some action she was at rest, not thinking beyond the moment. Not like Maureen who was aware of the potentialities at any instant, aware of herself, aware of all that might happen next, and already deciding what she would do about it. Doc Cassandra was unconcerned with future possibilities. She waited without tension, receptive but not concerned, content to see what would come.

"Ask Miranda his reasons, Mr. Shaw."

Miranda Mills had changed her clothes. She sat on one of the studio couches with her legs drawn up under a voluminous blue wool skirt. Only a pair of black boots showed. Her arms were wrapped around her legs under the skirt, and her chin rested on her drawn-up knees. Her long, black hair had been brushed, and the cuts on her hands were healing. The bruises on her face stood out. Different earrings dangled from her ears, but the same amulet hung around her neck against a thick blue turtle-neck sweater. Her large eyes in her pretty face watched me.

"Protecting me, I suppose," she said in a small, light voice. "Jerry doesn't talk much to establishment people."

"Where is he, Miranda?"

"At the camp, I suppose. We must have passed."

"You've been at the camp in New Park?"

"Jon was dead."

"Can you tell me what happened?"

"I don't know what happened, not much of it. Poor Jon."

Doc Cassandra said, "I think he wants to help, Miranda."

The luminous eyes focused on Cassandra Kingsley. I had the feeling that Miranda was a controlled girl, too, certain of herself. A certainty that did not come from experience, as Cassandra Kingsley's confidence did, but from some natural, intuitive strength. She was a girl who would do what she decided she had to do.

"Tell me what you know about Jon Calvin," I said.

"Oh, God," she said, almost a whisper.

She took a deep breath, let it out. She moved her head back and forth like someone trying to escape invisible chains. "He tried to kill me. I guess he tried to kill me."

"In the river park?"

She nodded. "I thought he'd gone crazy, some kind of urge, you know? We walked to the river, and he grabbed me. I didn't know what he was doing. He hit me with a rock. I ducked. There was no one around. I got away. He fell down and I ran."

"Why did he want to kill you?"

"I don't know. I don't know for sure he did, maybe it was a mistake. I thought he wanted . . . you know. I told him he didn't have to knock me out. He was scared. I smelled it, sweating."

"You don't know a reason?"

"No. He didn't even talk. He was shaking."

The knuckles of her scratched hands were white where she gripped her calves.

"Tell me what you know about Jon Calvin," I said.

She closed her eyes. The room was dark now, no one making a move to turn on the lights. "We were in high school together. We knew each other, that's all. He was popular, played football, liked dances. I hated all that. We had an honor club for the boys, the Longfellows. They had to be over six feet tall, be on a team or in a club. Jon was proud of being a Longfellow. They sort of ran the school, organized everything. They always wore suits.''

"After high school?"

"I went to Oregon. When I came back I couldn't live at home. Jerry was in New York, so I came down. After a while we all wanted some space, some air, so we built the camp at New Park. I knew some land we could get cheap."

"You met Jerry Levine in Oregon?"

Cassandra Kingsley said, "As I told you, Jerry was also one of my students. My first fling at being a guru."

"And Jon Calvin?"

"He went to Syracuse," Miranda said. "I didn't know that, of course, but we met him a few months ago in New Park. He was taking some business courses and coaching part-time at a private school. Jerry said he was like a big, shiny whale on a beach looking for an ocean."

"Jerry has a turn of phrase."

"He writes sometimes."

"What does he do most of the time?"

"Works on our houses, hunts, makes our shoes. We're making a community. We want to live with each other, not on each other."

"No work for money?"

"Sometimes, when we need money."

Doc Cassandra said, "They don't even pretend to be part of the society, Mr. Shaw."

I was getting a picture of Cassandra Kingsley's role: a kind of Delphic oracle. She stood against the door and made her comments on the action, like a Greek chorus of one.

I said to Miranda, "How did you end up in that park?"

"Jon began to come to the camp. He didn't fit, no one liked him. But he kept hanging around. I thought maybe he was mixed up, trying to find himself. I tried to help, no matter what the others thought."

"What did Jerry think?"

"We have to help each other. We're people, not personnel."

"Bravo," Cassandra Kingsley said.

Miranda didn't seem to hear her in the dark room. She was

all in shadow now, only her big eyes catching light from the street. "About a week ago Jon came to the camp acting funny. I mean, he wanted me to meet him in town. He acted, you know, interested in me. He never tried to make it with me before."

"A week ago? You're sure?"

She thought for a moment. "No, only about four days. It's all been so . . . fast. Just four days ago, I guess."

"He acted like he wanted to make you?"

"I told him I didn't feel like that. He went away, but next morning at work he was kind of wild. He left early. Then he called me. He was all shaken up. He said he had to see me alone. He asked me to meet him in New York. He told me to go down and call him at the Hotel Emerson."

"And you did? Why, if you didn't care about him?"

"Care?" she said. Her big eyes looked at me as if I were some strange animal. "Of course I cared."

"All right, what happened?"

"I got down about four o'clock and called him. He said something had come up, he'd call me later. I gave him the number of Carl's Tavern. Doc Cassie and I went there, and he called. I took a taxi to the park and met him. We went into the park, and . . . He must have been awful sick."

I waited, but she didn't go on. "That was about six P.M.?"

"I guess so. It was dark. I ran away."

"Why didn't you get a cop?"

"Police?" she said, stared. "He was sick, he needed help."

"What did you do?"

"I got a taxi outside the park. I was okay then, so I waited in the taxi to see what he was going to do. He came out of the park after a while, and he got a taxi. I was afraid for him, so I followed. He went to that building near Park Avenue. I waited outside. Then . . ."

She began to rock where she sat in the dark room huddled in her ball with her hands clasped around her legs under that voluminous blue skirt.

"You saw him fall?"

"I heard that awful scream. I ran around the corner. He was there in the street. People were all running. I couldn't move. I mean, I was asking why, why? I mean, was it me? I

# THE FALLING MAN 51

just stood there, and the police came, and the ambulance, and all sorts of people, and then I saw you and I ran."

"That was two days ago. Where have you been?"

She looked at me across the dark room. "He'd tried to kill me. I mean, maybe he had. Then I thought he'd killed himself. You know? I walked around most of the night. It was all so stupid. Near morning I got a bus to New Park. Jerry wasn't at the camp. I waited, but he didn't come back, so I took the Volkswagen and came down again. I must have passed Jerry on the road. He had the pick-up truck."

She fell silent. Doc Cassandra had no comment. It was quite a story. The question was: how much of it was true? All? Some? None? Two full days, almost, since I had seen her on the street. Two days of wandering, or two days to cover up?

"He was nothing to you, Miranda?"

"No."

"Yet you came to meet him."

"Yes, of course."

"You both worked at Stanniger Surveys last week?"

"We needed money at the camp."

"You know that a survey report was tampered with?"

"Mr. Stanniger talked about it."

"Did you see Jon doing anything odd, suspicious?"

"No, I just do my work there."

I went to her, leaned over her. "He tried to kill you. You say it wasn't personal. But there had to be a reason."

"I don't know any reason."

"Damn it, a man doesn't try to kill for nothing! He had to be desperate. Some big reason. Murder, Miranda!"

She only shook her head, not looking up at me. Her head moved back and forth, back and forth, in a kind of trance.

At the door Cassandra Kingsley moved, said: "You think Jon Calvin tampered with that report? You think Miranda knows why he tried to kill her? You think she's lying?"

"I don't know what she's doing," I said. "He worked hard to get her alone. He made sure he wasn't seen with her. He didn't want anyone to know he was even in New York. He picked the park, the river, and a rock, to make it look like a mugging, maybe. He had some reason for killing her."

"Did it have to be a rational reason, Mr. Shaw?"

She was a smart woman. No, it didn't have to be a rational reason. Maybe Jon Calvin had been sick.

"She better stay in town," I said. "The police will want to talk to her. Miranda?"

The girl did not hear me, or she didn't respond.

"She'll stay, Mr. Shaw," Cassandra Kingsley said.

She left the door and went to sit with Miranda. She put her arm around the silent girl, protecting.

# 16

IT WAS DARK, the cold drizzle falling, but Maureen had a dinner conference. I drove uptown through the wet mist that hung over the city diffusing all the lights, making the city and the people look like a strange, translucent world at the bottom of a hazy sea.

No one was waiting for me in the dark office this time. I dictated my report on Miranda Mills, and called Lt. Baxter. He was not on duty yet. I reported my talk with Miranda, and told them to pass it on to Baxter in case he wanted to see her.

I tried to get Thayer again up in New Park. I got no answer from his motel room, nor from the Stanniger Surveys office. I tried Max Stanniger's home. Stanniger was there, but Thayer wasn't.

"He said he would work on Jon Calvin's movements, and on Walter Tyrone of Hudson Furniture," Stanniger said in that crisp yet soothing voice.

"What's he doing on Tyrone?"

"I don't really know. Your Mr. Thayer is a close man. I don't even know what he's thinking, much less doing."

"If you do see him, or hear from him, have him call me."

Stanniger said he would, and then I left a message with our answering service to have Thayer call me.

I went home. Maureen was not there. You pay a price for being married to a successful actress, but there are advantages. She is rarely bored, and her complaints are not directed at me. I settled for another night at the television, and tried not to think about Jon Calvin. There are times when you have to let it lie fallow.

Maureen swept in, excited, just after nine P.M.

"Paul! Remember that wonderful part in the Samuels show? The one I didn't get? They're in trouble in New Haven!"

"Is that good?"

"Perfect! It's my part that has them worried! Angela doesn't like it after all. Samuels wants me to go up tomorrow. I'm to see it, then talk to him and the director, Nick Garburg. Can you come with me? You're the only one who'll tell me the truth."

"New Haven? Why not, baby? Thayer can handle it all for a day or two."

She whirled off her mink and did a sweeping turn. "Isn't it wonderful! A part with teeth! I know I'll be perfect in it, but you'll tell me, right?"

"Don't I always?"

She ended the whirl, dropped the mink to the floor, stood facing me. "Always. From the first day. I don't listen, but you tell me, and right or wrong I know you always will."

"I'm usually wrong," I said. "That's why you're the artist and I'm the detective."

She was on her knees, her head in my lap, her eyes looking away toward the window. "But you're my standard, the place I can stand on and relate to. When you tell me, then I can start thinking it out. All the auditions, Paul, remember them? I do, every one. I never could see myself until you told me what you saw and then I could see it all clear, even when you were all wrong."

"It's called perspective."

"Someone who tells the truth," she said. "I miss those days, Paul. When it was all art and no business. I miss the pizza for dinner; red wine for a party. I didn't even know how to say what lasagna tasted like until you told me what it tasted like to you. You were wrong, but it got me started."

"The hell I was wrong. You've got the palate of a whale. I don't miss those days. I wasn't sure of you then. I was all ambition and no excitement. Now you're good, very good, and you're mine, and that's exciting, and New Haven it is."

"One day at least. I like to show my detective husband. You can look at all the pretty young girls."

"It's not the young girls you have to worry about," I said.

She moved, raised her head, sat back on her feet like a temple supplicant. "Is that a warning, darling?"

I laughed. "No, baby."

But had it been? I didn't know. What I knew was that as

we talked about the old days, and our needs, and excitement, Cassandra Kingsley was suddenly in my mind.

"I don't know," Maureen said, her dark Spanish eyes deep and clouded, very female. "I haven't been very eager since you got back, have I? My mind, it gets so busy. There are so many things in my mind, you know? Too many things that shut you out. I'll make it right. Now, darling. Come on."

She stood, went into the bedroom. I finished my beer, and listened to the soft, sliding sounds of her clothes against her skin. The telephone rang. I swore at Thayer. But it wasn't Thayer. It wasn't anyone.

"Hello?" I said. "Hello?"

Silence. Every minute in New York they come to someone— the silent calls with only breathing on the other end. The line went dead. A crank? Or was someone finding out where I was?

"Paul?" Maureen's voice was soft. I went in to bed.

The silent call rang in my mind. I could hear it ringing and ringing. Then I woke up with the telephone beside the bed ringing. The clock read 1:10 A.M. I grabbed the receiver.

"Mr. Shaw?" the distant voice said.

Cassandra Kingsley. Did I glance at Maureen who was peacefully asleep?

"How'd you find me, Doc?" I said.

"I got your service. I told them it was urgent."

"Is it urgent?"

"She's gone, Mr. Shaw. And there's something else."

"I'm on my way."

I got up and dressed. As I knotted my tie, I stopped. Could I have handled it by telephone? I hadn't asked. Before I left I kissed Maureen where she slept.

# 17

SHE HAD CHANGED her clothes. She wore a full, white robe of the kind worn by Franciscan monks in summer. A robe that did much more to me than the tightest slacks could have. It told of an unhindered body; soft, ready.

"Come in, Mr. Shaw."

I looked around this time. She was alone. She lighted a cigarette. It was the nearest thing to a sign of agitation I had seen her show.

"Miranda's gone?" I said.

"She went for a walk. I expected her back here hours ago. Her car is gone."

"She knew she should stay in town?"

Cassandra sat down and crossed her legs. They were fine legs. She smoked in short, hard puffs. She was unaware of her legs, or my eyes.

"She knew," she said carefully. "It didn't appear to worry her. We went down to Carl's to eat after you left. We met a group and stayed to talk. She didn't say much. She did speak of Jerry a few times, rather oddly."

"How was it odd?"

"As if she was worried about how he was going to react to something. But I could be projecting my thoughts onto her."

"What thoughts?"

"I think she's pregnant."

I could hear Thayer chuckling—look for the obvious. A pregnant girl; Jon Calvin doesn't want to marry; he steals the poll data for the money to fix it; Miranda rejects the money and fixing it; so Jon tries to kill her. Classic, Thayer would say—with a smile.

"You're sure, Cassandra?"

"There were small things she said, and how she looked undressed. Perhaps four months."

"Jon Calvin?"

"I don't know that," she said. "There aren't any accidents anymore, Mr. Shaw, not for a girl like Miranda. The pill has changed all that."

"Not an accident, so not two people in the same unwanted boat. She had to have planned it?"

"I'd say so."

"Jon Calvin had no money I know of, no position, and his father's a foreman in a furniture factory. Not much of a candidate for pressure, unless she has other reasons."

"Miranda thinks in her own way."

"Okay, you were at Carl's."

"We came back here about eight o'clock. A Lieutenant Baxter from the police was here. He asked her about Jon Calvin, and she told him what she told you. He asked her to go in and make a formal statement in the morning. We talked for a time, mostly about ourselves, but impersonally. She's a fine modern dancer, well-trained, but now she doesn't really want to do anything but live out in those woods. Then, about nine-thirty, she said she wanted some air, perhaps stop to talk with some friends, and went out for a walk. By midnight I became concerned. I looked out and saw that her car was gone. I waited for over another hour before I called you."

When she finished she crushed her cigarette in an ashtray and lighted another. For her, it was like seeing a violent turmoil inside her. Her story was loose, with no hope, or risk, of substantiation. Miranda was simply gone. Maybe a pregnant Miranda—or was that all some kind of smokescreen?

"Could she be mixed up with my survey report?"

"Not from anything she said, but she has strong views. Those young people don't always think too clearly."

She was hedging. Deviousness was not her way, she was out of practice. Unless she was even more subtle, and was leading me up a garden path. I didn't believe that. You have to feel that you know when you can believe a person. But she was hedging.

"You wouldn't have called me so fast over just a hint of trouble," I said. "You'd have let them work it out."

She unwound herself from the chair with a flash of full thigh, and strode to a low cabinet near the front windows.

She opened the cabinet, looked back at me. I went to the cabinet, and bent down. It was a liquor cabinet. On the bottom, against the back, was a plastic-encased, miniature radio transmitter just larger than a cigarette package.

"Before I called you, I needed a drink," she said. "The Scotch in front was almost empty. I got a bottle from the back, and found that."

The transmitter was a professional tool, but the placement was amateur work. A liquor cabinet is a poor hiding place, it's used too much, and the transmitter had simply been rested behind a bottle. It could have been found at any time. Maybe my unseen shadow was not a professional after all.

"I hadn't gone to the back for a week," Cassandra said. "The bottle in front was full then."

"He couldn't know I'd be here, so it wasn't me he wanted to hear. You, or Miranda, or both."

"Why?"

"To hear what you said. To find out something."

"But I don't know anything about all this."

"Miranda does. She has to. Jon Calvin wanted her dead. Whoever put this bug here heard all we said earlier. Wherever Miranda is, I don't think she's alone. The question is, did she go away on her own or under pressure?"

The implication lay there in the room like a thick presence. Two A.M. is the beginning of the only slow hours the city knows, and outside the closed windows the noise and movement had faded to dying murmurs. Was Miranda part of a crime, or was she a prisoner?

"What do I hope?" Cassandra said. "Rogue or victim?"

"That depends, doesn't it?"

"It's not an easy choice when you care about someone."

We stood there near the windows. A few distant sounds reached into the room from the dark city. She brushed her cheek with her hand, smoothed her robe.

"Would you like a drink?" she asked.

"No, not now. Where would she go, Cassandra? The camp and Jerry. Where else?"

"She has a lot of friends scattered around. She could be anywhere, right in the city. She has only one relative, her father. The Honorable Benjamin Mills, from some political office he held once. He lives in Kingston."

She went and rummaged in an old roll-top desk. She wrote

an address on a slip of paper and handed it to me. I put it into my pocket without looking at it. I was looking at her in that white robe. She watched my action as if it told her something. I suppose it did.

"If you go to the camp," she said, "Jerry can be violent."

"All men can."

She smoothed the robe. "Or they wouldn't be men. A small violence at the right time."

"Good-night, Doc," I said.

When I was at the door she spoke behind me.

"Paul? Tell me what you find. Call me."

I nodded. I went down to my car. The rain had stopped, the mist was lifting, and a sharp chill of winter was in the air.

# 18

THE INTERROGATION ROOM was dim, bare, its walls invisible in heavy shadows. Like a dungeon deep inside a silent fortress, a room without hope, which is what it was intended to be.

Down the precinct corridor a drunk sang in the tank. Marsh Baxter straddled a bare chair across the bare table from me. "You think she's skipped out?"

"I don't know, Marsh. She's just gone."

"What do you want me to do?"

"If she skipped she's scared of something she knows. Maybe Jon Calvin's death wasn't so simple. If she didn't skip, then someone took her, and in your town."

"Can you trust this Cassandra Kingsley? She looked like an odd-ball to me. Do you take her story?"

"I don't know that either. Right now I trust her, I have to."

Baxter rocked in the chair. "You like her, Paul?"

"I like her."

"She's a looker. That why you have to trust her?"

"That's why I don't know."

"Tough. Maureen's nice."

"Maureen's nice," I said.

"This Kingsley could be covering for the girl, or herself. Leading you a chase. The girl could be cold in the cellar; in the river."

"You want to look around?"

"Okay, Paul. I'll put a bulletin out on the girl. I'll have the precinct down there check out Kingsley and the building. If Miranda's in the city, we'll find her, cold or kicking. Now what about this guy who's been on your back?"

"He's strong, quick, and knows what he's doing. He's had me pegged for two days and I haven't smelled him. The way

# THE FALLING MAN 61

he's acting I think there's some information floating around loose, and he wants to find out if I know it. My hunch tells me Miranda knows it. He bugged the apartment to try to find out if she talked about it. She didn't talk about it. Now she's gone. I got one of those silent calls around the time she took her walk. I think he was making sure I was out of his way."

Baxter scratched at his jaw, his eyes flat the way all policemen's eyes get when they are thinking in front of an outsider. They carry a weight, the police. What they do can mean life or death for people they have never met. The drunk still sang, loud and mindless, in the detention tank.

Baxter said, "That Jerry Levine was tailing Eric Calvin and MacDougall?"

"There's too much action for a nothing report."

A high, anguished scream echoed from the squad room. A manic scream of despair, chopped short. I waited in the silence for the scream to sound again. It didn't. In the dim interrogation room there were only small, nameless noises like rats scurrying inside the walls.

"What does Thayer say about it?" Baxter asked.

"He's in New Park. I can't reach him."

"You couldn't reach him the night Jon Calvin died."

"No."

"How long have you worked with Thayer, Paul?"

"Long enough."

"He was on the case first, wasn't he? He was up there in New Park before you came back from L.A."

"Yes."

"The kid came to your office, searched. He knew your office was on the New Park case, he had to. He didn't know through you. I don't see a sharp operator like Thayer getting spotted by an employee in a job that almost had to be inside, not if he was just investigating."

"You don't like him, Marsh."

"I don't like him. He'll do anything that's good for Thayer if he can get away with it," Baxter said. "That shadow who's been on your tail seems to know a lot about you. He was at your door before you even knew who Jon Calvin was. Where is Thayer right now, Paul? You don't know, do you?"

"He's in New Park."

"You're sure?"

I said nothing. How could I be sure?

"You don't know what it's all about," Baxter said. "Maybe Thayer does."

"I'll ask him," I said.

# 19

DAWN COMES SLOW to New York in November. I hadn't been able to sleep. Maureen stirred beside me.

I got up and made some coffee. The cook would come in soon to start breakfast. Maureen believes in a solid breakfast to raise her energy fast. I drank the coffee at the kitchen window. It has a view of tarred roofs, Hell's Kitchen, and the river sullen in the distance. The sun was up before I woke Maureen.

She did not open her eyes. "Hello, darling."

"I have to go upstate," I said. "Sorry, baby."

Her eyes stayed closed. "Again?"

"Again."

"You can't come to New Haven. Your work."

"I made some coffee."

"Bring me a cup, okay?"

I brought her a cup. She sat up against the headboard, and opened her eyes. She tried to keep the anger from her voice. New Haven meant a lot to her.

"You couldn't postpone it one day? Come up with me, see the play, tell me how great I'll be in the part?"

"How long will you be in New Haven?"

"I don't know. Three days."

"I'll try to join you, baby."

"When do you have to go?"

"Now."

In the living room I called our answering service. Thayer had not checked in. I had another try at his motel in New Park. His unit didn't answer. I packed a bag, dressed in my proper gray tweed suit, and strapped on a small shoulder holster. My working pistol is a light Colt Agent with a two-inch barrel, six shot. I put extra cartridges in my bag, called Thayer again.

There was still no answer from his unit. I told the motel manager Thayer could be in trouble, and would he check the unit? Thayer wasn't in his unit. I called Cassandra Kingsley. I felt a surge of adrenalin. Do we all thrill to the lure of adventure?

Her phone didn't answer. I dialed again. No answer.

I closed the bag, slipped on my topcoat, and went to the bedroom. Maureen was drinking her coffee.

"You look handsome," she said. "Why didn't you have the talent?"

"I have talent, baby, in another art. I'll call you at your hotel in New Haven."

"All right, dear." She drank coffee. "Paul? You had a call last night. You went out."

"Part of the case I'm on."

She nodded. Her eyes watched me, asked for details. Only her eyes, not her voice. I didn't have to lie about the details, not with words.

"I'm sorry you have to go," she said after a moment. "We're apart so much, aren't we? Both of us. I know I'm so often apart even when I'm not away. I'm here, but I'm not, am I? I'm on some future stage, in some play I want, my mind in another person's body—the stage role. I don't think about you enough because you let me relax with you."

"That's good, baby," I said. And it was good, that warm cave where two people can relax and not think about each other every second, tight and nervous. But we were not relaxed now. Cassandra Kingsley was there, even though Maureen didn't know her name or face. There, Cassandra, like a lump between us.

"Remember the first time I went on the road? You said it was okay because it was us against the world. I wanted to go away that time, did you know that?"

"Of course, baby," I said.

"I wanted to go, and I wanted to come back," she said, finished her coffee. "Be careful, Paul. Come back."

"I'll be careful," I said.

"If you didn't come back, where would I have to rest from it all?"

"I'll come up to New Haven if I can," I said.

"I know you will," she said, and smiled as I left.

In the car I pushed through the heavy morning traffic as

fast as I could all the way to number 124. I ran up. There was no answer to my ringing. I went back down and routed out the super. He was in his pajamas and primed to swear me blue, but I beat him to it. In our country, sadly, most poor people fear the police. For me that has its uses.

"Open the top front. Cassandra Kingsley," I snapped. I flashed an old special police buzzer, and let him see my gun. The standard intimidation. With enough urgent arrogance, and early in the morning, it usually works.

"I knew that one was trouble," he grumbled, and got his keys.

Upstairs he let me in. The apartment was neat and empty. There were no signs of a struggle. Her make-up and toothbrush were gone and the sheepskin boots were not there.

I went out without another word to the super. Would it change what was building in me for Cassandra Kingsley if, in the end, she was part of whatever had really killed Jon Calvin? I hoped it would. I hoped I had some sense left.

I headed north up the West Side Highway. I drove fast. A voice whispered of my job, Maureen, John Thayer, and in the sunny morning I knew I was on a highway that could become a disaster course.

# 20

THERE IS ONLY one fast, direct route from New York to New Park—the Thruway. If Miranda had returned north, she would almost certainly have used it, as I was using it. After crossing the river at South Nyack, I stopped at every gas station on the Thruway. There aren't many.

I asked the same thing at all of them, "Two women, one driving a gray Volkswagen, muddy. Long black hair, a big wool skirt, blue. An amulet," and I went on to describe Miranda in every detail I could remember. Then I described Cassandra. "The Volkswagen girl would have gone through about anywhere from ten P.M. on. I don't know about when the other one would have passed."

I changed the time minimum for Miranda depending on how far along the Thruway I was. I didn't know what kind of car Cassandra Kingsley drove. I got nowhere. Until the next to last station before the exit for New Park.

"I don't know, mister," the attendant said dubiously. "I think maybe the Volkswagen could have stopped here last night about eleven P.M. Gray, muddy, a New York plate. I remember 'cause it came in fast as hell, and damn near stalled. The girl didn't even get out. She was a looker, and dressed funny. Like she had something hanging around her neck."

"Was she alone?"

"Far as I know. Seemed like she had a load in the back. Drove out fast, too. Burned rubber, if she's the one."

"How about the other one? The older woman?"

"Nope, no one like her. 'Course, I only remember the *cars* good. You don't know what car she was driving?"

"No," I said, "and thanks."

That was all, and I left the Thruway at New Park.

The massive, gray Catskills loomed to the west. Old mountains, worn down and no longer jagged crags, tamed by time. But under the rolling gray skin of the winter trees the rocks were still there. Did you know that there are more rattlesnakes in New York State than in Texas? We live in a strange country, only partly tamed and half understood.

Thayer had picked a quiet motel on the edge of the town. I told the manager in the office I would share the unit. He was uncertain. He was young, with a beard, but no swinger.

"I dunno, mister. How do I know it's okay?"

I showed him our card. "I'm Shaw, we're partners. We're up here together. If he doesn't want me with him, I'll move out."

"Detectives? I don't want no trouble in my place."

"Who does?" I said. "Let's have a key."

Thayer had taken the last unit—away from the road and hidden in trees. It was a typical motel room; modern, shiny, with a tile shower, and furnished with the tasteless neutrality that passes for designer modern in Grand Rapids. They all look the same now, the motel rooms. Like bad model rooms from a second-rate modern art museum whether they are in Medicine Bow, Montana, or on the outskirts of Boston.

Thayer was not there, and neither was his car. The bed had not been slept in. That made me stand and stare at the bed for some time. Then I unpacked, hung up my extra suit, put my shirts and underwear into the drawers, and looked the room over more carefully.

Thayer's toilet articles were in the bathroom. His extra clothes were there. His bag was unpacked, and his pistol was not there. His tool bag was gone. His receiving equipment was always in the trunk of his car. I searched the whole room: closets, drawers and under the beds. I found two telephone numbers on a pad. The first was Stanniger's home number. The second I didn't know. I dialed it.

"Hudson Furniture, good morning," a girl's voice said.

I hung up. Cars passed out on the road. I dialed Max Stanniger's office and asked for him.

"No, Mr. Shaw, I don't know where Thayer is," he said, his voice cooler, edgy. "I think he should have contacted me by now."

"He will," I said. "Anything else I should know?"

"Angus MacDougall and the boy's father have been in

raising hell. MacDougall doesn't think much of our security, and they both want to know if I have any proof that Jon Calvin tampered with the report. Of course, I don't, do I? It puts me in a poor position, Mr. Shaw. MacDougall's hinting he might get the whole study rejected. We're about ready to present it to Regent-Crown."

"We'll come up with something," I said.

"You better, Mr. Shaw, and soon."

He hung up and let the threat hang. It was getting touchy. I called our answering service in New York. They had not heard from Thayer. Where the hell was he?

It was a good question, and I had no answer. I went out, got into my car, and drove on to Kingston. At Kingston Police Headquarters they told me that the address I had for "Assemblyman Mills" was out in Wayne Center. I drove on west toward the mountains through a series of suburbs and villages until I passed a small, discreet sign that announced: Wayne Center. On the same roadside stanchion was the warning: Speed—25—Limit, Laws Strictly Enforced.

I slowed to thirty M.P.H., and drove through the residential parts of the town. There were a lot of trees, lawns, park-like areas. At first there were new tracts on both sides of the road; well-laid-out tracts with houses a cut above most middle-class tracts and some attempt to differentiate the houses. Then the tracts disappeared, and the houses became bigger, older, with more land and a sense of having been there on their tended grounds for a long time.

Most of the old houses were painted white, or were brick with white trim. They had fanlights above the doors, Colonial columns, aged shutters and widow's walks, large garages and antique hitching posts in front under the sidewalk trees. Solid old houses where people had lived for many generations. Part of the land, sunk into it and growing from it, not sitting on top of the land as if the first wind would blow them away like the endless ranch-style houses of the tracts in California.

I reached the "town" and realized that Wayne Center was all residential area. A rich, preserved village, zoned against the modern world of industry and commerce, the zoning ruthlessly guarded. The town itself looked like a restored New England village, all the shops disguised as emporiums of a bygone time. Police Headquarters was a discreet, red brick building that looked like a library.

# THE FALLING MAN

I asked the desk officer how I got to the address Cassandra had given me for Benjamin Mills. He looked me up and down.

"You have business with Assemblyman Mills, sir?"

In a town like Wayne Center the main job of the police is to protect the leading citizens from annoyance. Paid watchdogs in the service of citizen privacy and privilege. I was well dressed, so he had to be careful.

"I'm investigating his daughter. Paul Shaw, private investigator from New York."

His eyes told me that I had just taken three strikes by my own admission: investigating, private and New York. He'd have learned it all anyway, and I had an ace.

"You better talk to the Chief," he said coldly.

"How about talking to Sam Norman?"

"You know Sam Norman?"

"That's right."

Just when he had been anticipating the fun of watching a city sharpie put on the merry-go-round, I had struck him a low blow—local influence. He picked up the desk telephone. When he hung up he didn't even look at me. I was still a slicker, and from New York, but no more fun.

Sam Norman appeared from a side corridor. His tall, whiplike frame was more stooped than I had remembered, as if he was near-sighted. On duty he wore a shabby black suit of some iron-hard cloth intended for use not show. The small eyes in the craggy deacon face peered at me as he ambled up.

"Shaw. What brings you up here?"

"Same case. I'm looking for Miranda Mills."

"Won't find her here. She didn't stay around after she got back from college. Try New Park, that camp."

"I will, but I want to talk to her father anyway."

"Why?"

"I'm not sure she wants to be found. If she doesn't, she won't be at the camp. I want to know where she might go."

"She's run off?"

"She's gone, anyway."

"She don't get along much with Ben."

"He's her father."

Norman chewed on his thumbnail, his sharp eyes considering me. "Yeh, I guess he is. Okay, Shaw, I'll take you over. Ben Mills can be touchy with strangers."

Outside in the sun he led me to a dusty black Ford. It had no markings, no identification, except the give-away buggy whip aerial. He drove along the main road for about a mile toward the west, then turned off into a blacktop country road. Along this road the houses were, if anything, bigger and set far back from the road in wider grounds.

"Know anything about Ben Mills?" Norman said as he drove.

"Only that he's an Assemblyman."

"Was," Norman said. "Once. Two years, that was it. He was sort of young then, he got popular with the Italian vote in Kingston."

"Then he got unpopular?"

"You might say," Norman agreed. "Got caught taking a little money from the wrong company."

"Graft?"

"That depends. A fee for work, nothing exactly illegal. The company happened to be in a strike with a union was about ninety per cent local Italians."

"I get the picture. He never ran again?"

"Nope. He switched sides, since he was out with the dago vote anyway, and took up lawyering for local businesses. He got pull up in Albany, got appointed to a few jobs. Once you get with that Albany crowd, they take care of you."

"Is he a crook?"

He glanced at me, sideways, and looked back at the road. "You don't hear me say that. He never been indicted, if he did have to beat a couple of grand juries. We near nailed him once, over in Kingston." He was driving slow, telling me about Mills. "I ain't seen him in court in fifteen years, but he made enough to move out here ten years ago. Inside tips, I figure, what to buy up and where to sell it. That's how you get rich in this kind of territory. He bought up a lot of the right land before the Thruway come. Did okay, I guess."

"Is that what you nailed him on, almost?"

"We figured he was helping out a gambling joint. We never proved it, only he didn't sue us, neither."

"A sharp dealer who doesn't much care how he deals, that it?"

"If that's how you see it," he said.

He speeded up then, and silently watched the big houses pass along the quiet road.

# 21

THE HOUSE WAS gray Victorian Gothic, had three stories, and was hidden by trees on grounds larger than Washington Square. The garage had space for six cars, but held only one big Lincoln. There was an atmosphere of neglect.

No, not neglect, emptiness. The Lincoln shined like a diamond alone in an empty room, and the rest of the garage was littered. Near the house the grounds were manicured, but the distant rose garden was overgrown. The upper story was shuttered tight, the house was overdue for paint, yet the front door brass gleamed. It made me think of a busy mansion after the family has died, or moved away, leaving one last survivor, and not enough people to fill it or keep it up.

"He lives here alone?"

"Always did," Norman said, "except for the girl and a couple of hangers."

A gray-haired woman opened the door. She took us through a big living room into a front study. The living room had it all—cabinet hi-fi, color television, grand piano, a wall of best sellers, air conditioning, sleek coffee tables and mammoth couches, wood that glowed with wax and rare grain—but it was in the study that Benjamin Mills lived.

"I'll tell Mr. Trevino you want to see Mr. Mills," the woman said.

There was another color TV in the study, facing a big leather chair that was used a lot. The desk was littered with papers and law books. An old safe stood between battered filing cabinets. There was a wall of law books, state statutes, bound legal and news magazines. Another wall was all framed photographs of posed groups. I recognized some of the faces; national politicians. Norman pointed to a thick, dapper young man dressed in a conservative black suit of twenty years ago in one of the pictures.

"That's Mills. The other guy was a Senator."

Mills was in almost all the framed pictures. Those he wasn't in were autographed with some message of appreciation to him. I was reading the inscriptions when the man himself appeared in the study.

"Hello, Sergeant. You've been a stranger."

He was still thick, had grown solid, and was no longer young. A heavy, coarse face and expressionless eyes clashed with a nervous mouth. A sense of power was weakened by more than a hint of wariness. He was a man with some position, even authority, who knew too well how thin the ice could be. His suit was still black, and still conservative, but the cut was today and the soft cloth was rich.

"I keep pretty busy, Assemblyman," Norman drawled.

"Sure, sure," Mills said quickly. "Well, what can I do for you and Mr. Shaw?"

The woman had told him my name, and he had come in with it ready. A man who lived on a smile and the right words at the right time and place. Behind him in the living room a swarthy man sat on a couch watching us. His face was alert but placid, like a watchful dog. This would be Mr. Trevino, the right-hand man: assistant, confidant, major-domo, errand boy, and, if necessary, muscle man. Smart enough, loyal, proud to be on the inside with his boss.

Norman leaned against a filing cabinet at his ease, watched Trevino with a thin smile, and answered Benjamin Mills without looking at him, "It's Shaw's show. Talk to him."

Annoyance pinched the one-time Assemblyman's thick nose, but the automatic smile was in place when he turned to me.

"Mr. Shaw, then."

"I'm looking for your daughter Miranda, Mr. Mills."

"You don't look like her type."

"Her type?" I said.

"Anything in pants dirty enough and lazy enough."

"I'm not after her skirt, Mr. Mills, just some talk about a case I'm on. Has she been here today or last night?"

His eyes remained expressionless, but I sensed all his muscles tense under the five-hundred-dollar suit at the word "case" like a hound at the call of the hunting horn. It was partly simple reflex, he'd spent his life in "cases" of one kind or another, and partly the sensitive nose of a working wheeler-dealer. I had the impression that Benjamin Mills's fingers were never idle.

Norman said, "Shaw's a detective, private. He's working on some trouble down at New Park. Outfit named Stanniger Surveys. You wouldn't know about that, would you?"

"I know the Stanniger outfit," Mills said. "What kind of trouble?"

"You don't know about it?" Norman said.

"No, I don't," Mills snapped.

I said, "They had a report stolen."

Norman said, "Someone looking for an edge, a fix, maybe. That's your line, right, Ben?"

"I'm a businessman, Norman!"

Norman smiled. Mills turned to me. His coarse face was impassive, but there were sweat beads on his brow.

"What's all this got to do with Miranda?"

"We're fairly sure who actually stole the report," I said. "He's dead. Someone had to have paid him. Miranda was involved with him. Now she's missing."

"Dead, huh? So look for a live one, a man. You'll find her."

"A kid named Jon Calvin," Norman said. "Know him?"

"No."

"Where would she go besides the camp or here?"

"I don't know."

"Special friends? Relatives?"

"None I know."

"You can't tell us anything?"

Mills glanced around the study as if he were looking for Miranda. He looked out toward the shining living room. He went to his desk, opened a cedar box, took out a thin cigar, and offered the box around. I shook my head. Norman didn't make a move. Mills closed the box, lighted the cigar.

"Even in high school she didn't act like other kids," Mills said, his poker-eyes still showing no expression. "On her seventeenth birthday I tried to give her a car. She said she didn't need a car. Not didn't want, didn't need. She could walk, I should give the money to someone who needed it. My money! She brought tramp kids home like stray dogs. She'd stay away for days, and I'd find her in some community room with ten others."

"Anyone special?" I asked. "Do you remember?"

He shook his head, barely hearing me. "It wasn't what some people say about me, no. That I'd understand. Kids don't know how the world is. They have to grow up and find out. But she never seemed to care about how I made the money. She acted like there was no difference between me and a factory hand."

Norman snorted in the corner. Mills didn't hear him anymore than he had heard me.

"You know what she called me? A victim. When she came back from Oregon she said I was another victim and she couldn't be alive here. I was 'a prisoner who identified with the existence imposed on me.' I couldn't help it, she said, I was indoctrinated by the conditions I was born to."

Norman's laugh was mocking, cynical. I couldn't tell if the skeptical laugh was for Mills or Miranda or both. For me, what Mills was saying sounded like Miranda all right, and like Cassandra Kingsley.

Mills waved his long cigar. "I'm a victim chasing like a drooling dog for things I don't need or want. That's what she says. I can't reach her. I never will. I know what I want, and I've got it. Look around this house. I've got it all, and I've got it because I want it. No one manipulates me. What are they all talking about? I don't know. I've tried to listen to her, understand what she means, but I know I wanted everything I've got, and I know no one makes me do anything."

"She thinks we're all prisoners, Mr. Mills. Of a system we think is natural, but isn't. She wants to free us, and I think it's those ideas that got her into this trouble."

He crushed his cigar less than half smoked. "No, I know what got her in trouble. No morals. She never had any morals from the start. When she was fourteen she was going out her window. No morals, no principles, and the rest is cover-up."

He looked down at his ruined cigar. "Her mother tried before she died. I tried. I never looked at another woman, not when my wife was alive, and not since. The minister tried. I made her go to church to learn. I sent her to good camps. She was an animal in heat all her life, dirty-minded. Now she's mixed up with a crook you say. I'm not surprised."

He believed it. He believed he was a moral man with right principles he lived by, and in his world it probably hadn't been easy when willing females wanted something from him. He was proud of his moral strength.

"So you don't know where she'd go, or anything about Jon Calvin and her?"

"She didn't come to me. I never know her studs," he said bitterly. Then he stopped, looked at me. "Calvin? Eric Calvin's boy? Regent-Crown Furniture?"

"You do know him?"

"I go to MacDougall's company picnics. MacDougall gets too close to his shop people. I remember Eric Calvin has big ideas for that boy of his. Sent him to college."

"No more," Norman said. "The kid's the corpse."

"That's too bad."

Norman came out of the corner as if bitten. "Too bad? That's the word? You garbage! I'm listening and I ain't heard nothing. Shaw don't know you. So you ain't close to your girl-kid? She's a tramp? You're a tramp, she's your kid, she's tied in something got more smell than flowers, and when I see her in it I got to see you somewhere. There's a dirty buck around, and that's your game."

"Lay off me, you cheap muscle-brain!"

I watched Sam Norman's face turn into a mask with only the small eyes still moving. He stepped toward Mills. His hand came up, flat and open, back to strike. His teeth grated in his thin mouth.

"You know them all, mister: Stanniger, Regent-Crown, Walter Tyrone at Hudson, Eric Calvin, the boy, that gang of nutty kids. You know every angle from Albany to the city line. That camp your tramp-kid got going, it's on land was yours, check? They maybe paying you off with a deal? There got to be a pay-off, and I'm gonna find it."

I'm not sure Mills heard anything. His eyes were fixed on Norman's raised hand the way a paralyzed bird watches a cobra ready to strike it. Fear in Mills's eyes, and fascination. His mouth was wet.

I watched, waited, and Trevino was there.

The swarthy man pushed between Norman and Mills. He held a length of iron pipe that must have been inside the wrinkled suit that would never hang right on Trevino's work-muscled shoulders and ease-grown belly. Norman stared at the pipe, breathed.

"Call his Chief, boss," Trevino said.

Mills didn't answer. His thick body, in a five-hundred-dollar suit, was backed all the way against a wall. He still stared at Norman's raised hand. His tongue, small and pink, licked out between his lips.

Norman looked only at Trevino, at the iron pipe. He breathed through his nose with a faint whistling sound.

Then he walked past Trevino and out through the living room. I followed, conscious as I passed of all the shining possessions of the thick man back there against the wall of his study.

Outside, I found Norman leaning with both hands flat on the hood of the car. His face was turned away from me toward the east. He breathed slowly, deeply.

I waited, lighted a cigarette and smoked in the sun. Norman's head moved to follow the flight of a drab bird I could not name. The bird flew out of sight. Norman shuddered.

"I hate slime like him. Too dirty to be honest, too yellow to do anything big."

"He's afraid of you."

"I worked him over. That time we almost nailed him in Kingston for fronting the gambling. I worked him over hard. Put him in the hospital for two months. We didn't get him."

"You got away with it?"

"It was too near a miss, he couldn't afford trouble. Anyway, a beating like I gave him does something to a man." His voice had become dispassionate, matter-of-fact, like an engineer analyzing mathematics. "He never been the same, not around me or any other cop. A man doesn't forget when he has to take that punishment."

"You think he had something to do with Jon Calvin?"

"I don't know. Depends on how much is in it. He's still tougher than he looks except with me. I'll drive you back."

We drove back to the library-like Police Headquarters. I got out, thanked him, and started for my car. He came along behind me.

"Where to now?" he said. "That camp?"

"It's the only lead I have to her."

"I better go along. It's out of my territory, but the New Park boys know me. They don't much like New York private operators, either."

I said, "You wouldn't want to keep an eye on me, would you?"

"Yeh," he said, grinned. "I would."

"That's what I thought," I said. "Okay, you lead the way."

On our way south I stopped at the New Park motel. Thayer hadn't returned or called in. I didn't want to think of what Baxter had said. But couldn't help thinking how much more Norman seemed to think there was going on than Thayer had suggested.

# 22

THE CAMP WAS at the end of a dirt road four miles off the county blacktop highway and five miles west of New Park. A rocky section of low hills, scrub trees and tangled undergrowth worked by loggers over a century ago and forgotten. From the highway to the camp there had been only two farmhouses, both dilapidated and surrounded by rusted junk and rotting debris.

There were seven shacks set haphazardly on the slope of a hill, and a long, low structure in the center. The shacks were unpainted, built with new boards, old boards, doors, sheets of tin, tar paper, auto bodies, logs, plastic and other materials I couldn't name. They were dirty, the ground was a quagmire of mud after the rains.

"Junk, but solid," Norman said, as we crossed a footbridge over a small, clear stream.

The shacks were insulated and weatherproof, and the ground was mud but there was no debris. Board walks had been set on the mud between all the buildings. There was a community pump, and clean backhouses behind each shack. Electric wires ran from a low hut that had to contain a generator. Behind each shack was a vegetable garden, bare now, but dug and tended and ready for spring. There was glass in the windows—clean glass with curtains.

Norman pointed. "They've got a smokehouse, too. Good one."

Four of them appeared in front of us as we left the bridge. Two long-haired young men in buckskin and beads like Indians, and two girls in shaggy skirts and wool ponchos. They were alert, and had heard Norman talking.

"Surprised, Sergeant?" the shorter of the men said.

"Yeh," Norman drawled. "You won't get froze or washed out."

"No burden to the community, Sergeant. We don't plan to commit suicide. We intend to bury you instead."

"You wouldn't be a bad kid, Berger, if you didn't have such a big mouth," Norman said.

I said, "You two know each other?"

"Yeh," Norman said. "Mr. Berger and me had a run-in last year in New Park."

"A small demonstration," Berger grinned. "The local fuzz called for mercenaries from the adjoining territories. The good Sergeant was forced to put the arm on me."

"How long they hold you?" Norman asked professionally.

"Too long. The matter is in litigation."

"You're funny," Norman said. "Someone said you got a law degree."

"You didn't come to discuss my legal training."

"We want to see Jerry Levine," I said.

"Second house on the left."

Levine was working on some shoes. He looked up at us, but went on working. His hair was combed and his mustache was neat, but he did not look like he had slept much. His workbench took up all of one wall of the main room of the shack. It was an all purpose room—double bed, rough dining table, Salvation Army couches and chairs. The only other room was a kitchen. There was electric light and a big, potbellied stove that glowed.

"You want something, Shaw?" Levine said.

Norman stationed himself at the door. Jerry Levine glanced at the Sergeant, but went right on working on his shoes. There was an open notebook beside him. Against the far wall, near the bed, a row of clothes hung on an iron pipe. Most of the clothes were female. I recognized the red and black cape Miranda had worn the first time I saw her. I nodded to Levine's notebook.

"Writing?"

"I put down my thoughts. I think a lot when I'm working."

"You're comfortable here."

"We do all right. You find Miranda?"

"Yes," I said, "and lost her again."

"She moves around."

"Is she here, Levine?"

"No."

"Have you seen her since last night?"

"No."

"But she lives here, right?"

"She lives in this house," Levine said, hammering at his shoes. "I missed her in the city. She hasn't come back here."

"Do you know where she is?"

"No. She goes where she wants."

Norman snorted from the door. "You shack up with a girl, and you don't care where she is?"

Levine looked at Norman. "Who's he, Shaw?"

I introduced Norman. Levine seemed to study the tall figure and craggy face of the sergeant. Then he went back to his shoes. "You keep your women on a leash, Sergeant?"

"If I got to," Norman said.

"I'm sorry for you," Levine said.

I said, "You lied about not knowing Jon Calvin."

"It was none of your business. I didn't lie about not knowing what he was up to. I still don't know."

"You can't tell me where Miranda is? Or Doc Cassandra?"

"No."

"You must know her friends where she might go?"

"She does what she wants. You don't get help from me."

"Do you know Miranda's pregnant, Jerry?"

I watched him as I said it. He didn't answer at once. He hammered three nails, hard. One after the other.

Levine said, "Is she?"

"Would it be Jon Calvin's, Jerry?"

"Ask her."

Norman snapped, "We're asking you."

"I wouldn't know."

"Were you jealous of Jon Calvin, Jerry?"

He hammered four more nails in quick succession. There seemed to be an echo, and through a window I saw men and girls working on the next house. They sang while they worked. One tall boy sat against the house and played a guitar:

*"This land is your land, this land is my land,*
*From California to the New York island;*
*From the redwood forests,*
*To the Gulf Stream waters,*
*This land was made for you and me."*

Norman went to the window to watch the work and the young voices singing. Jerry Levine hammered another nail, examined the shoe he was making.

"I don't know anything about Jon Calvin," he said.

"Where'd you go from Cassandra's place Sunday?"

He worked for a moment. "I didn't go. I hung around. I went out looking for Miranda. Yesterday, too. Then I came back up here, went out hunting. We needed meat."

"When did you get back here?"

"Five, five-thirty."

"You hunt at night?"

"Why not?"

"So you were alone? No one saw you?"

"No witnesses."

"How well do you know Eric Calvin and Angus MacDougall?"

He hesitated only a second. "I don't know them."

I let the lie rest there. He could worry about how much I knew.

Norman spoke from the window: "She's run off with some new boy."

"If that's what she wants," Levine said.

Norman watched the workers outside. "Just like that? I don't believe you, boy. It ain't human, not if you're a man."

"Whatever you say, Sergeant," Levine said.

Norman still looked out the window. One voice sang above all the others: high, joyous, abandoned:

". . . *every time I read the papers*
*That old feelin' comes on——*
*We're waist deep in the Big Muddy*
*And the big fool says to push on.*"

Norman turned to look at Jerry Levine. The long-haired youth continued to hammer on his shoes.

"That kid on guitar," Norman said, "he's high."

"No," Levine said, "only turned-on some. Once a week, grass or acid. Maybe a benny or two."

"You admit it? Marijuana? LSD?" Norman snapped.

"You'd say we were if we weren't. Everyone says it. What difference does it make if I admit it in private?"

"It makes a difference if I come down on you," Norman said.

"You're out of your territory, you've got no warrant, and we don't drop acid in camp. This place means a lot to us. Until it's legal, we don't keep any junk here."

I said, "You got this land from Miranda's father?"

"It's on record."

"How did you pay? Some favors for Ben Mills?"

Levine laughed for the first time. "Cash, man. Hard cash for Mr. Mills, and a note with only fifty per cent higher interest as a show of love for Miranda. Money isn't the hang-up here."

Norman turned now, leaned with his back against the wall beside the window. He studied Jerry Levine.

"Why don't you work, boy?" Norman drawled. "None of you kids is dummies. What do you get? Women, that I can figure. Easy women, fine, but there got to be more in it for you."

Levine stopped work. "What do you get? Paid to protect a world isn't yours. What are you when they retire you? A shell. Your work means nothing. A slave. Just making a living takes your soul."

He was hacking again with those short word blows, chopping at the wilderness he saw.

Norman shrugged. "Guys break laws, I stop 'em. The laws are there. A guy breaks the law, he gets punished. That's my work."

I said, "What do you want from life, Jerry?"

He picked up his shoe, considered it. "You ever read about the planet Neptune? We discovered it in 1846. It's so far out it won't be back where we found it until 2011. It sits out there in silence, and takes almost one hundred and sixty-five years to go around the sun once. Three generations of us live and die in one year of its time. My whole life, even if I'm lucky, is one half a Neptune year. A blink of time. I don't want to find out the day I die that I've never lived."

What did I say? I thought of Neptune out there, a planet neighbor as space went, and I wouldn't live to see it go around once.

Norman had an answer. "Get what you can," Norman said.

"Mine?" Levine said. "Get mine? That's what they want

# THE FALLING MAN

me to do, Sergeant, just like you. That's the big trick. They need personnel and consumers, not people, and the technology shapes our lives and our minds to make us what they need."

"Most people seem to like what they are, son," Norm said.

"Most people are walking carrots," Levine said. "I want to exist. Right now that means own nothing, and drop out."

"Hell, boy, I been protecting them walking carrots a long time, and I don't own nothing. That don't mean a man don't do his job all the way."

"You?" Levine said. "You're something else. For you it's being a better man than anyone else. You're tougher and smarter, the best man. That's how they play you. Do your duty all the way."

Norman smiled, but it was a thin smile. I guessed that Levine had hit him close to home. Their eyes locked for a long beat. Levine did not back down. Neither did Norman.

"We'll be back, Jerry," I said. "If she shows up, tell us."

He didn't answer. I wasn't going to get anything more from him. Not now, and not with Norman around.

# 23

WE STOPPED AT New Park police headquarters, and Norman went in to find out where Jon Calvin had been living in the town. So far, Miranda was a dead end, and maybe we could pick up her trail through Calvin's past actions.

Norman came back out in a hurry. "There's trouble over near Calvin's room."

"What kind of trouble?"

"Don't know. Cops here just got a call that way."

He drove to a quiet street on the edge of town with me behind him. It was a street of trees, large old houses with Room-for-Rent signs, and yards in the state of disrepair that always comes when former homes become rooming-houses. A dead end street, with a wide vacant lot beyond the dead end overgrown with a jungle of dry winter weeds under tall trees. The lot was not empty now.

Police cars were parked at the dead end. There was an ambulance. The usual curious civilians who seem to come up out of the ground itself were there. They craned to watch a knot of police, ambulance attendants, and one gray-haired civilian gathered some sixty feet inside the overgrown lot.

"Calvin lived over there in number twenty-six," Norman said, and pointed to a big house with outside stairs that led up to open galleries that surrounded each of its three stories.

In the vacant lot, as we approached the knot of police, one of them turned to stop us. He recognized Norman, and Norman paused to talk to the New Park cop. I went on to where the ambulance men were bent over something that moved on the ground.

It was John Thayer.

I held to a tree. I had to. I would have fallen, my legs gone to jelly.

# THE FALLING MAN

The thing on the ground was Thayer, my partner. I held down the nausea, tasted it in my mouth and fought it down.

Thayer lay on his right side, half over toward the overgrown ground. He moved. A slow crawl toward something he could not see, like a smashed animal crawling to some unknown instinct.

His face was a mass of dark, dried blood. I saw the faint glint of an eye, one eye. The bridge of his nose came through the dried blood like a raw, white bone. His suit was torn and caked with dry blood. His left arm dragged limp, a boneless thing of rubber. I could see the points of bone under his sleeve where the upper arm had fractured and torn through his flesh.

His left leg trailed loose as if no longer part of him. Fluid bubbled and whistled in his throat as he breathed. His breathing was slow, careful, and yet I knew that he was not aware that he breathed at all. One ear was torn, and his mouth was a dark hole in the caked blood. Even his teeth were black with the dried blood. Each inch he moved, he moaned to some inner pain.

The ambulance men were trying to hold him for the gray-haired civilian to examine.

Each time a hand touched him, he shrank back an inch and whimpered like a beaten puppy.

Each time the hand was withdrawn he began to crawl ahead again, an insect moving by inexorable purpose toward some goal he could not know but only sense he must, somehow, reach.

Each time someone spoke near he moaned, and tried to crawl in a different direction, and each time he crawled again in the same direction, his body unable to move in any other path.

"John?" I said, bent down.

Under the blood his head turned, slowly, cocked as if trying to understand what it was he heard. Uncertain of what he heard.

"John? It's Paul. What happened?"

He crawled, stopped, and his head went down to rest in the grass.

"He can't hear you," the gray-haired civilian said. "Just sounds, no words. His ear drums may be damaged."

"You're the doctor?"

"Coroner."

"Are you going to stand and watch him?"

His eyes drooped like a sleepy drunk. "Who're you?"

"Paul Shaw, his partner."

"I'm figuring how to move him," the Coroner said.

A police captain with a notebook came up to me. "I'm Captain Katona, Shaw. Was Thayer working on anything besides the Stanniger matter?"

"Not that I know. He was in touch with you?"

"Only when he arrived yesterday. He reported in like he did the first time he came up. He tell you anything?"

"I couldn't reach him since he left New York yesterday. His bed at the motel wasn't slept in. No messages."

The Coroner said, "That figures. I'd say he's been like this maybe twelve hours. In and out of consciousness all night. He's tough, crawled all the way from over there by inches."

The Coroner waved toward a place in the tall weeds some sixty yards away near the road on the far side of the vacant lot. The weeds were flattened there, and a trail led straight to where Thayer lay now. I could see him, broken and semiconscious, crawling all night and into the morning, dark or light meaning nothing to the pain of his brain. And as I thought, saw the endless night, Thayer raised his head again—slowly, in agony—and began his terrible inching crawl once more.

"We've got to move him," the Coroner said. "Boys, bring a stretcher. Move him easy."

The two ambulance attendants brought the stretcher, and picked Thayer up. He screamed.

A long scream of naked agony—and fear.

He squirmed in the hands of the attendants, tried to escape, his darkened brain knowing only that hands had beaten him, and afraid of any hand with the mindless reflex fear of a hurt animal.

"Hold him, damnit!" the Coroner cried.

The attendants sweated, held. Thayer lay on the stretcher, held down, breathing in great, shallow gasps. The hollow of his blood-caked mouth moved:

"Tyrone . . . at . . . Tyrone . . ."

His body went limp. My stomach dropped. The Coroner bent over him, straightened up:

"Passed out again. Get him in the ambulance."

# THE FALLING MAN

Mopping his face the Coroner climbed into the back of the ambulance with Thayer. It drove clanging away. Norman came up.

"Know what happened, Katona?"

"A kid found him not fifteen minutes ago," Captain Katona said, "saw him crawling. His car's over on the other road. Jon Calvin lived there in number twenty-six. Shaw says he wasn't on any other case. No evidence around, not a hair. He was beaten with more than fists, but we didn't find a weapon."

I went to the spot where Thayer had fallen first. Norman was behind me. There was a lot of blood, and the tall weeds had been trampled by more than one set of feet. I could find no weapon.

"Must have taken it with him," Norman said.

"Something handy, like a jack handle," I said. "Twelve hours he was lying here!"

"Guess someone didn't want him snooping around," Norman said.

They were getting ready to move Thayer's car, hold it for evidence. There was no blood in it. And no gun. Whoever had beaten Thayer had taken the gun. There was nothing in the car that told me a hint as to what had happened. All his tools were missing, too, except the receiving equipment in the trunk. That was still in the trunk.

"His equipment's gone," I said.

"Valuable?" Norman asked.

"Valuable enough. He wouldn't leave it, unless he had been tailing someone. A quick tail from wherever he left his tools."

"How about money, Shaw?"

"He carried money, not that much. A thief doesn't beat a man like that. He hits and runs."

The New Park police took the car away. Norman and I went across the lot to our cars. I followed him to the hospital. The Coroner had gone, and a busy surgeon had no time to talk. I asked him what he thought about Thayer, and he just looked at me.

"We're operating in ten minutes. If you're a religious man, try praying. I don't know how long it will take. I don't know all that's wrong."

He was gone. We found Thayer's room, but they were already wheeling him out. He was no longer moaning, was barely breathing, and as he passed under the white sheet the full impact hit me for the first time. They had cleaned up his face, and I wished they hadn't. The blood had covered the ruins of what had been Thayer's cool, alert face.

I began to shout there in the corridor. I raged. "The animal! What kind of animal beats a man like that! The filthy cretin! Why? Who beats a man like that!"

Nurses came running. I pushed them off. Who? Who beat a man and left him to crawl in a vacant lot for twelve hours? Two interns came. Norman grabbed me, and with the interns, pushed me along the corridor until we reached the door of an empty visitors room. Norman got me through the door, closed it against the interns, and held it closed with his back. I stood crouched in the room ready to hit him. His small eyes were down to slits as he watched me.

"You want to calm down?" he said.

"Go to hell! You hear? I'm going to crucify the man who did that."

"Sure you are," Norman said. "Not here."

I took deep breaths, trying to calm, filling my lungs with great gulps of air. "How?" I said. "What animal?"

Norman watched me. "You finished? Got it all out?"

"For now," I said, nodded. "Okay, for now."

"Okay," Norman said, and his thin lips curled into a snarl. "Now you listen to me. What the hell do you think you're playing at, Shaw? You think you came up here for some kind of high school hockey game? You expect polite competition? Come and investigate us, Mr. Shaw, we'll play the game fair and square!"

He glared at me out of those small, bright eyes. He was shaking now, and so was I, but I stood there in the small and silent visitors room and listened to his voice come low and hard. The lines in his craggy deacon's face were like etched steel.

"You've been around the city too long, you hear? All nice and legal, writs and court orders, every crook has his lawyers. You think you're dealing with international diplomats and their armies, Shaw? This is our life, mister! You come poking around, and you know what you're poking into—the whole damned world for the people up here, their lives all the way! People don't play polite in a place like this, Shaw, they

# THE FALLING MAN

don't play by any rules except survival! They got hate in them, Mister Shaw, and they got a lot of iron!"

He stopped, patted at his pockets for a cigarette and he didn't find one. I gave him one of mine. I had stopped shaking. I was listening to him now. He lighted the cigarette.

"Let me tell you about Ben Mills, just for a picture. I told you about working him over that time? I worked on him with everything I had for six hours. I hit him everywhere'd make a bruise. He didn't break once. He just took and took. I never got to him, never made a dent in anything except his hide. You know why? Because the gambler who was the only one who could finger him was missing. If we didn't find the gambler, and Mills didn't break, he was clear. So he took my best. We found the gambler four years later—in Moon Lake. It was just chance his body ever floated up.

"The charge we had against Mills was nothing, maybe a year. But he'd have been out in the cold up here. His edge would of been over. And Mills ain't so special. He's tough, but our plain businessmen can be tougher. Why you think we get a high percentage of fights, beatings, murders? In the city you get slick crime, money crime. We get power crime, men fighting each other for the edge. For you this is all a fee, a puzzle, and a few years in jail for the guilty. For people up here, it's their whole world you're shaking!"

When he stopped, the sounds of the hospital returned as if from a distance. The heels of visitors, clicking. The voices of nurses. Rubber wheels that squeaked. A machine pumping somewhere. The indifferent voices of two doctors discussing golf.

"So you think there's more to this than one kid out to make a few dollars?" I said.

"Maybe."

"Thayer mumbled about Walter Tyrone."

"If there's a big money angle, it could be Tyrone. Or Mills. Anyone who needed an inside edge."

"Any ideas about what the money angle could be?"

"Not a one," he said, shrugged. "Maybe that Mills girl can tell you. Maybe you can find what Calvin did with the report. You know how to work, Shaw."

"It's your territory," I said. "Where do I start?"

"New Park isn't my territory. I'm off-base here."

"Unofficially, then."

He thought for a time. "I figure the girl's part of it. She's Ben Mills's kid. She's on the run, or someone shut her up. That's a hard road. I'd find who Jon Calvin sold the report to."

"The weakest link?"

"That's what I'd do. I backtrack the kid, if I'm doing it."

It was good advice, and it was Norman's backyard. He was on duty, and I promised to call him later. Before I left, too, I asked about Thayer again. He was still in surgery. I went out feeling sick. But the human being has amazing resilience. I was hungry. I had two hamburgers by myself.

# 24

TWO MUSCULAR COLLEGE-BOY types played with a football in front of where Jon Calvin had lived. They stopped to stare arrogantly at me. I was a square in a city suit. They could take me anytime.

A frail old lady answered the door of number twenty-six. "You're new at the college? I may have a room soon."

"No, ma'am," I said, and showed her my license. "I'd like to see Jon Calvin's room. Did he have many visitors? Any girls?"

"His father, some boys. No girls, poor boy," she said.

"No girls at all?"

"None. I noticed. It was odd, you see? I don't mind them having girls in discreetly. It's quite natural."

The room was on the second floor with an outside entrance from the gallery—an advantage I hadn't had in my college days not very long ago. The old lady opened the door and went away. She had her own sense of discretion.

It was a clean room, with a neatness that came from a housekeeper not a tenant. The furniture was the usual: a bed for sleeping; a desk for studying; a table for eating; two stuffed chairs for talking; a couch for visiting. A normal room in a rooming-house where college men lived. Except that the room was not quite normal.

There was a feeling of emptiness, of not being lived in for some time. All was in order, and a thin film of dust had settled since the last cleaning. The film of dust had not been touched by anyone living in the room, but it had been disturbed—lightly. The room had not been lived in for a week, but it had been searched. A careful, expert search—the way John Thayer would have searched.

And there was a sense of something missing, something

not in the room that should have been. A mark of individuality. Jon Calvin had brought nothing of his own to the room. There were books, yes: shelves of books and notebooks and papers, but nothing else, nothing private. Not a piece of furniture that had not come with the room. I was sure of it. Not a chair, stool, ashtray, trophy, keepsake or framed photograph. Nothing from home. No past.

A transient room, temporary. Jon Calvin had been passing through on his way to somewhere, or he had wanted to believe he was only passing through this small stop. A room as transient in its way as that brief cubicle in the Hotel Emerson.

I crossed to the shelves of books. There were novels: all recent best sellers, book club editions. They had been read more than once each, and passages were marked in the margins with one, two or three vertical lines. The marked passages were all epigrammatic; the kind of short statements a man could toss off at the right moment at a party.

Slim volumes of love lyrics: simple, old-fashioned and passionate. The undying love of the strong man, and the good, pure woman.

After the novels and the lyrics it was all business.

With a pattern that emerged as I slowly read along the shelves.

Solid, difficult, diamond-hard books on the managerial revolution, the corporate state, the techniques of industry. The histories of big corporations: General Motors, Ford, IBM, DuPont, the rise of Xerox. The biographies of tycoons; their hard, single-minded work and their luxurious lives. The autobiographies of smaller men who had risen from low to high, and how they had done it—the principles of their personal triumph, and how anyone could do it by following the same principles that ranged from shrewd business tips to always sleeping with two windows open.

Books to improve reading skill, improve decision-making, improve judgment, improve clarity of speech. Ten ways to sure success; seven ways; three ways. A book on how to appraise management in ten easy categories. Stock market schemes, investment systems, and cheap tracts for shortcuts to the money top.

Finally, current management magazines and the textbooks for his courses. His notebooks and papers. The courses were elementary accounting, office procedures, and direct-mail selling techniques. The notebooks, and the papers, were cut and slashed in the red ink of the instructor. The prose of his notes was tortuous, poor, misspelled.

His grade report, slipped into a notebook, showed that Jon Calvin had not been a good student. Average.

I sat down in the neutral, empty room, and the pattern fixed itself in my mind. A descending pattern. The managerial revolution, to inspiration, to elementary accounting. The corporate state, to self-help, to direct-mail selling. Dream to reality. In a single transient room.

A depression settled on me. I sat, lighted a cigarette, and blew slow smoke into the sad room. As sad as the cubicle in the Emerson, maybe sadder. In the Emerson I had sensed the sadness of romanticism and desperation. Here there was only the longer sadness of a misspelled dream—the eager hopes of a bright, handsome blond youth. What had Jerry Levine said? A shiny whale on a beach looking for an ocean.

Jon Calvin had found only a swamp. Why?

I stubbed out my cigarette in one of the anonymous ashtrays of the silent room. I searched. The closet was full, Jon Calvin had not stinted on clothes, and no man is consistent all the way. His dreams may have been of J. P. Morgan, but his clothes were the dashing, loud clothes of a young man. The drawers of his bureau contained all the accessories—*Playboy* fashionable, from bizarre cuff links to tasseled shoelaces. His shirts were mostly French-cuffed, striped and white, and not cheap. His underwear was brief, low-cut and tapered as if he always saw himself undressing before a lady who would be impressed by his lean body.

The camera was in the bottom drawer under three cashmere sweaters. A mini-camera, the master-spy bit again. Not a new camera, well-used, and designed to take microfilm shots in sharp detail. The camera was in a leather case for carrying, and there was a tiny, plastic canister beside it.

The film was in the canister. A developed roll of microfilm negative. I took it to the light. It was a series of typed sheets, a document. I could not read it, and there was no magnifying glass in the room anywhere, but it was filmed documents. I had no doubt that it was the Regent-Crown survey report.

In his bureau drawer.
Undelivered?

I searched once more. I turned out everything this time, looked under everything. The scribbled note was slipped under the desk blotter: the name Tyrone, and a telephone number I now recognized—Walter Tyrone's Hudson Furniture Company. There was, of course, no date, and the writing was a vague scribble.

# 25

WALTER TYRONE STOOD. "Who the hell are you?!"

He was a rawboned man with a broad Irish face and the gnarled hands and loose frame of a peasant. His business suit was sloppy as if he wished he didn't have to wear a suit. His office was for work, not show. The furniture was gray metal, and the office was cluttered like the back room of a busy shop. The windows overlooked the dark November river.

"John Thayer's partner. You remember John Thayer?"

"Yeh. I remember him," Tyrone said. "Out!"

A female secretary and a door guard hovered behind me in Tyrone's office. The guard moved closer. I dropped into a crouch, ready. I was in no mood to hold my temper. I hoped no one tried to throw me out. I wouldn't be much use in a Kingston jail.

"He just pushed in!" the secretary said, shocked.

The guard waited for a definite nod from the boss. He was smaller than I am, but his eyes glared with the hate of a man fooled at his job.

"I want to talk," I said. "I don't want to wait."

I was breathing hard. I had parked near the factory, in a rundown section of narrow sloping streets and old blackened brick buildings, like a hundred other riverfront areas up and down the Hudson. Factory towns built a long time ago when American industry had started, and most of the towns were backwaters now; but the Hudson Furniture factory was bustling.

The receptionist had called Tyrone. He wouldn't see me, no appointment. I was angry by now, damned angry. I said something brilliant like "Appointment, hell!" and was up the stairs before the door-guard knew what was happening. I went past Tyrone's secretary at full speed.

"Call your army," I said, "or throw me out yourself. You look tough enough."

"Don't try to kid me, mister," Tyrone said.

"Then talk! Someone almost killed Thayer!"

His blue eyes darkened like a cloud. "Sit down."

He waved the guard and the clucking secretary out. The guard didn't like it, but he went. The secretary closed the door. Tyrone leaned back in his swivel chair.

"Talk, Mr. . . . ?"

"Paul Shaw. Was Thayer here last night?"

"Late, about ten P.M. I was working late."

"Did he walk out, Tyrone?"

"He walked out."

"I'll find out," I said. "He's not dead yet."

"Find out then, and be damned!"

His broad peasant face was red, and his pale eyes popped with anger. He had a temper. He was not a man who had come to the top of his company by way of the country club. We glared at each other like two prize bulls. I was doing it all wrong, but I could see nothing in my mind but Thayer crawling on the ground, whimpering like a crushed dog.

"What happened to your partner, Shaw?" he said.

I told him, in detail. He winced. For a split second I was sure I saw a flash in his pale eyes. Then they closed up.

"He's not exactly a tactful man, your partner. We have people up here who dislike outsiders meddling. I'm sorry."

"That's about what Sam Norman said."

"Norman over in Wayne Center? He should know."

"Do you know Jon Calvin and Miranda Mills?" I asked.

"I've met Eric Calvin's boy, yes. I hear he's dead. Some trouble about stealing a report Stanniger did for Regent-Crown. You're the one who killed him?"

"Yes. You know a lot."

"It's a small town up here."

"What about Miranda Mills?"

"Never met her. I know Ben Mills."

"How well?"

"Every businessman in town knows Ben Mills well."

"You talked to Stanniger's people about a poll like the one Regent-Crown hired?"

"I looked into it."

"That information would be valuable to you?"

# THE FALLING MAN 97

"If it helped me run my business. I decided it wouldn't. I could do my own thinking and forecasting."

"Or maybe you got the data cheaper and faster?"

He took the accusation like a stone. "If I was going to hire that report stolen, I'd have waited until Regent-Crown decided what they were going to do about the data."

"Jon Calvin had your name and number written down. He had the report to deliver. Those are facts."

"He never called me, or talked to me. That's a fact."

"And you wouldn't buy the report?"

"Hell, no."

"Then who would buy it?"

"Who knows? I run my own business. Maybe the kid worked on speculation, hoped to sell it. Maybe Eric Calvin was in on it. The kid gets the report, Eric listens at Regent-Crown for signs of what Regent-Crown decides to do. That might sell."

His telephone rang. I watched him become the smooth, crisp businessman. An ordinary businessman who made and sold furniture but who could casually brainstorm the idea of a devious theft. Was he speculating, so sure of himself he could toy with hints of the truth, or simply casting suspicions? Casting suspicion seemed to be a habit up here. I thought of Ben Mills, and of Norman's tirade. A small world where everyone knew everyone, but looked out only for himself.

Tyrone hung up. "Is that all, Shaw? I've got work."

"What did Thayer want when he came last night?"

"Same as you. He went to my house, damn him. My wife isn't well. I was working, so she sent him here. He barged in and just about accused me the same as you're doing. Only he was snottier, threatening, the big deal from the city!"

The picture didn't sound like John Thayer. Me, yes, under the conditions of Thayer in the hospital and a clear lead to Tyrone. But Thayer's way was cool, precise, businesslike.

"I told him what I'm telling you," Tyrone said. "Call the cops or get out! He laughed at me! Said he'd break me down! He knew how to handle hick crooks! So I called the guards, had him tossed out."

Tyrone's face was red with anger at the memory. Thayer had angered him, why? That wasn't John Thayer—unless he had been putting on an act. To smoke Tyrone out? Force a mistake, an indiscreet move? A telephone call?

"You called the guards? By telephone? Intercom?"

"Hell, no. I was too damned mad. I went out and got them."

"You left the office? For how long?"

"Couple of minutes. I had to go all the way down to the doors. I was steaming, let me tell you."

Not time enough to make a decent plant. I studied the office. The windows were locked, the office year-round air-conditioned. The windows were not sealed. There were heavy curtains.

"Were those curtains drawn last night?" I asked.

"How the hell do I know? Yes, I think so. They usually are at night. I like privacy when I work."

"So Thayer left with the guards? When?"

"About ten-ten, I suppose."

"You're sure the guards didn't work him over?"

"I'm sure," Tyrone snapped, and laughed. "They had him by the collar! It was a pleasure. I came back and . . ."

He stopped, his face going grim, looked at me. "Damnit, he got under my hide, but I'm sorry he was hurt."

In the silence I heard machines hammering somewhere. There was a steady pulsing throb that seemed to be part of the building itself. Outside, in the sun, steam drifted thick from the factory in the November afternoon air.

"When did you leave here last night, Tyrone?"

"Midnight, maybe a little after."

"Any special reason you worked so late?"

"A production and design problem on our new line. It had to be settled by the morning, or the pilot production line would have been held up days. It happens that way sometimes."

"A new line? Quality furniture, maybe?"

"That's right. It's the latest wrinkle in the whole field."

Maybe it was in the whole field, and maybe it wasn't. But a new line was what Regent-Crown had bought the report on. Tyrone had left this office at midnight—or a little later. Thayer had been beaten somewhere around midnight, if the Coroner had been right.

"Thayer was attacked around midnight," I said.

"That so? I said I was sorry."

"Tyrone . . ." I began.

He stood up. "Get out of here, Shaw. Now!"

I took out one of my cards, scribbled the name of my New Park motel on the back, and dropped it on his desk.

"Thayer came here for a reason," I said. "I'll find out."

"Then find out."

When I left, his eyes were turned down to look at my card that lay like a white germ among the important papers on his desk. He poked at the card with one finger.

I thought of Thayer's croaked words, "Tyrone . . . at . . . Tyrone."

# 26

SPYING AND DETECTIVE work need darkness. To most men the dark is an enemy, a time of terror waiting to pounce. Even in the advanced, civilized world. To a detective working alone to find what others do not want found, darkness is a friend, a time of relative safety from hostile eyes. But even a detective must sometimes stand exposed in the sun.

I left the office of Hudson Furniture, but not the grounds. It was not a defense plant in any way, there was no security beyond the few company guards, and they would not have orders to keep me out. Not me, no, only they would have orders to stop any unauthorized strangers. I was unauthorized, and I walked around to the rear of the office building feeling as naked and exposed as a prudish matron in a public dressing room.

Under the windows of Tyrone's office I was in the shadow of the adjoining building. That was some help. The factory yard was battered concrete, with a broad strip of grass between it and the building wall under the office windows. Evergreen bushes grew close to the wall. The bushes were thick, but I could make out a space of bare earth behind them.

Above, the windows of Tyrone's office on the second floor had old-fashioned, thick stone sills. The building itself had a flat roof above the third floor, with a parapet around the edges. An average man could easily throw a grappling hook up to the parapet and haul himself up to the second floor sill in seconds.

I found the tools behind the bushes. They were Thayer's. He had placed them carefully under a large, thick bush where they would have been invisible in the dark last night. His listening and entry tools. One miniature transmitter was not in its place. I knew where it was.

# THE FALLING MAN

The bushes showed no signs of a struggle, but the grass some fifteen feet away did. Not much struggle. A single patch of torn sod, some almost unnoticeable dried blood. Thayer's blood. There was more on the macadam at the edge of the grass. Two large stains. Tire tracks through them. The factory yard was littered with grease stains, oil leakage, chemical spillage. Who would notice two more stains in a factory yard?

*"Tyrone . . . at . . . Tyrone . . ."*

Thayer had been trying to tell me, anyone, that he had been hit here. Hit first here. There was not enough blood here, and too much in that vacant lot near Jon Calvin's room, for all of it to have been done here.

All that had happened was clear now. Obvious. Thayer's violent act upstairs had gotten Tyrone out of his office. Thayer had unlocked the window behind the curtains. He had gone down with the guards, and waited for Tyrone to leave. Tyrone had left at midnight, or just after. Thayer got into the grounds and climbed up into Tyrone's office to plant his transmitter bug. He had come back down.

Out of the night he had been hit, knocked out. On the grass, and dragged, bleeding, to a car. He had been driven to the vacant lot down in New Park, and there beaten savagely with some weapon—and with a cold, calculated ferocity. His attacker had then returned to Hudson Furniture, driven Thayer's car to New Park, and made his way back to Kingston once more to get his own car.

In the dark he had overlooked Thayer's tools.

Overlooked, or not bothered to remove the tools? I had begun to see a kind of pattern in all that had happened. A pattern of improvisation, rather than any long-range plan. Like mud thrown in handfuls at a fan, letting the mud splash everywhere at random.

# 27

"WHAT DO YOU know about Walter Tyrone?" I said.

Max Stanniger sat on the edge of his chair behind his desk. He rubbed his hands together as if he were cold. He had been a surprise when I had walked into his cubicle office in the jerry-built pre-fab. On the telephone his voice was tall, well-groomed, efficient, impressive. Here in his office, he was a small, thin man in a wrinkled suit. He had a pinched, rabbit face, and his lank gray hair was wispy over bald spots. Unimpressive, nervous, looking like a man who had never had enough to eat. Only his eyes seemed to fit the voice—cool and efficient.

"Not much, Mr. Shaw. He came up the hard way, I believe. Once worked in the factory he now runs. He went to night school, an ambitious man. He's done well with Hudson."

It was strange to hear that confident voice come from the shabby body. As if some powerful tycoon spoke through Stanniger's body like a ventriloquist through a dummy. Yet I sensed that it wasn't the voice, and the cool eyes, that were misleading. It was the scrawny, unimpressive outer shell. There was a quick and hard mind behind the meager façade. He was simply a man who spent his money and time on other things than his appearance, and relished his skill and power more than any reward.

"Would the report be valuable if whoever had it also had someone inside Regent-Crown to listen and look?"

Stanniger worried his small chin. "Perhaps. If the man knew what my report said, someone inside Regent-Crown could read the signs of what they planned to do. He would know what to watch for. That could be a distinct advantage."

"Would Tyrone gain from something like that?"

"I really couldn't guess, Mr. Shaw, but he might. Do you suspect Tyrone?"

"He was interested in your study, and Thayer mentioned his name. Jon Calvin had his name written down. He was the last to see Thayer as far as I know."

"Which is all very little," Stanniger said.

"Very little," I agreed. I took out the roll of microfilm. "Is this the report?"

Stanniger took the film, stared at it. Then, after a moment, he got up and left the office. I followed him across the main room of the pre-fab to a microfilm reading machine he used for his files. The four members of his regular staff watched us as Stanniger fitted the roll of film into the machine, turned on the viewing light, adjusted dials.

"This is it. Where was it?"

When I told him his quick eyes sparkled with relief.

"Still in Calvin's room? Then he never passed it on? That's wonderful, Shaw. It's all over. You did a fine job."

"I still don't know who hired him to steal the data."

"Does that matter now?"

He switched off the machine, pocketed the film, and led me back to his cubicle office. Inside he perched on his chair again. His rabbit face was deep in thought.

"No, the important part was getting the report back. Who cares who hired Calvin as long as I have the report."

"I care," I said. "Jon Calvin didn't beat Thayer to a pulp. Someone else did that. The same someone who, one way or another, sent Calvin to my office to be killed. The case isn't over until I know who."

He was thoughtful. "Beatings are part of your risk, eh?"

"Thayer's my partner, Stanniger. I can't let anyone get away with beating him."

"Perhaps true, but hardly my concern. I'm not paying you to discover who beat your partner."

I just looked at him. He didn't flinch a hair. Who had beaten Thayer was not his problem—not if he had to pay for it. If that was his real reason for ending the case now.

"I have another client who'll pay me, if that's what really bothers you," I said, "but I'm not so sure it's all finished for you anyway."

"But you found the film! He still had it."

"The place had already been searched once," I said. "I

think it was Thayer who searched. It might have been someone else, but I think it was Thayer, and he wouldn't have missed that roll of microfilm."

Stanniger's weak chin worked like a mouse chewing a bad piece of cheese. "Which means?"

"That the film wasn't there when Thayer searched. It was planted later, probably by the man who beat him and at the same time. Which also means the report was delivered, and then put back in Jon Calvin's room."

"To make us think it had never been delivered."

"That's what I see," I said. "It's easy enough to copy out some prints of the film. One print would do the trick for the buyer. He has his data, and he plants the film to throw us off."

Stanniger's piece of mouse cheese seemed to get worse tasting with each worried chew. "So someone has the report. All right, at least work until you're sure. What can I do?"

"Get the top Regent-Crown people here if you can."

He may have looked like a worried, shabby rabbit, but he moved, and thought, with the impressive efficiency that was in his voice. Within seconds he had called Regent-Crown, located the president, stated his case, and emphasized the urgency of the Regent-Crown men coming down at once. It was a fine performance, with just enough said, and just enough left out, to make the need seem maximum. He played the Regent-Crown president like a fish. When he hung up he had a satisfied smile on his face. He enjoyed his own skill.

"Half an hour," he said. "What do we do?"

"Wait," I said.

I smoked and relaxed in a hard chair not intended to induce lounging around. Stanniger did not relax. He was not a waiting man. His fingers drummed on his desk. The kind of man who had to be busy, must always have something cooking in his life to feel alive. I thought about Jerry Levine, Miranda, and Doc Cassandra—about what they would think of Stanniger.

"I simply cannot understand why the report is so important to someone," he said. He had to talk.

A man who had to be thinking or doing, forever busy. Busy for what? That was what Jerry Levine would say. Work just to work; to make more money he couldn't spend, didn't even need? Yet Stanniger was the kind of man who got things done in our society of two hundred million people, and would the different ways of Levine and Cassandra work in a society of two hundred million? I didn't think so, and neither did Levine or Cassandra. They didn't like, or want, a society of two hundred million. They wanted a smaller, quieter world. But societies change slowly, and men do not live long. Jerry Levine would not live long enough to see a smaller society that no longer needed men like Stanniger to function; and while he lived he had his own private needs, so he had to drop out if he was to live in the quiet world he wanted.

"The report seems important to you," I said. "Enough to hire us and try to find where it went, get it back. You seem to want to know what happened pretty badly. After all, you said yourself it isn't very important, you have copies, why worry about it so much?"

"That's an entirely different matter," Stanniger said brusquely. "I don't give a damn about the actual report, the data isn't really secret. But it is supposed to be private. I won't sell many studies if my data isn't guaranteed to reach the client first. At least I have to show them I'm trying to protect their study."

His fingers did their little drum-step on his desk. He frowned as if listening to some inner voice, and nodded to himself vigorously. He was approving the logic and determination of his course of action—if that was what he was really doing.

"Why would a company hire one of your studies in the first place?" I said. "What do they really gain?"

Stanniger arched an eyebrow at me. "What do you know about American business, Shaw?"

"It gives us more goods than most countries can have," I said, "and it's big and powerful."

"The main word is 'big,' " he said. "We're the richest country the world ever saw because our industry has the richest market ever known. We're all workers, producers, scientists, artists, plumbers, detectives and gangsters; but what we are to industry is consumers and nothing more. To industry we're all consumers; at home, and all over the world."

"I'm not sure I like being that," I said.

"You feel 'used'? A pawn? All right, we're 'used' in a way, and we 'use' other people and accept what we're born into, but life is short and maybe it's the best way after all. I'm not so sure most people want any other way, or could handle any other way. Maybe working for ease and security the short time we're here is our best way. Anyway, our industry made the single great discovery that has made us the rich, powerful people we are."

"What's that?"

"Volume," he said. "Profit doesn't depend on quality or price, it depends on the size of the market. The important factor in business isn't how good a product is, or its price, but simply how much of it we can sell. If you sell enough of a product, you can almost give it away and get rich. Not price, Shaw, but volume."

"So companies want to know how much the consumer can be expected to buy? How big the market will be?"

"Exactly. Once that was easy to know. Take-home pay was low, we knew a man would buy food, clothing, shelter, a little recreation. Now, with the necessities taking a smaller and smaller percentage, it's harder to know what the consumer will do with his money. The variables are almost infinite."

"Industry wants an edge like everyone else," I said. "They want to know what the consumer will do."

"They have to have the edge," Stanniger said flatly. "The volume of our sales has made us rich, but it brought its own problem with it. Everything carries its own negation in it, Shaw, its own special trouble. Volume sales means volume production. That means enormous investment, mammoth plants and machinery, and enormous loss if a mistake is made. So volume and giant investment mean planning—rigid planning."

"That's sort of a dirty word, isn't it?"

He dismissed that with a sharp wave. "Economic necessity has nothing to do with politics. Call it what you like, our economy is planned. Investment is too big, failure too tragic, to allow chance or the human element to prevail. Companies must know what the buyer will do, and if the answer isn't good, then they must manipulate the consumer, condition him to buy.

"That's where I come in. I try to tell companies what the consumers will do, and, later, to assess what effect their manipulation has had. I'm a specialist, and we're in an age of specialization. I'm trained to do what their own people can't do, help them know what they face in the market."

"It would also help a company to know what its competitor

is going to do, right? Another furniture company would like to know what Regent-Crown is going to do?"

"Yes, but the competitor would have to know a lot more than my study would tell him."

"Such as what Regent-Crown plans to do about the study."

"At least that."

"So an inside man is needed. Someone in Regent-Crown management?"

"An inside man, but not management," Stanniger said. "The last people who would need to steal my study are Regent-Crown's management. They'll see it within days, and they would know directly what they decide to do about it. No, if there is an inside man, it would have to be someone not in management."

I thought about Walter Tyrone, and an inside man, as we waited for the executives from Regent-Crown.

# 28

THEY CAME INTO the pre-fab like staff generals into an advanced outpost—looking neither right nor left, the importance of decision implicit in their every motion.

Angus MacDougall came second—the lower general. The leader was a slender man some few years younger than MacDougall. He had a sensitive face that had been hardened by command, but that had not quite lost the capacity to show the pain he had to cause by some of his commands. A Western face, in a way, like a cowboy turned into a businessman. He would have looked better in Levis than in his business suit and overcoat.

"How are you, Stanniger?" he said, and looked at me.

MacDougall said, "Shaw, our president, Mr. Hedger."

"George Hedger," the Regent-Crown president said, shaking my hand, and said to Stanniger, "What's our problem now?"

Stanniger explained what I had told him, showed the roll of micro-film to them, and repeated why I thought the film was meaningless. MacDougall listened, and nodded slowly to his inner thoughts. Hedger considered me speculatively.

"Then you think the boy delivered the data?" Hedger said.

"I don't know that, but I'm pretty sure the film had been planted back in his room after my partner searched."

"And Jon Calvin is dead, so there is someone else."

"Calvin is dead," I said.

"The poor fool!" Hedger said. "For what? How much could he have been paid?"

"The prime question seems to be why did anyone pay him anything?" I said. "Only just now I'm not concerned with why or how much. We'll learn that when we know who. Who paid him, who beat Thayer? What do you think about Walter Tyrone?"

"Tyrone?" Hedger said. "Impossible. No, never."

MacDougall said, "Tyrone's a tough man, George. I wouldn't think he would try anything like this, but he's capable of it if he thought it would give him a jump on us. I've heard Hudson was having a little trouble, and planning a new line."

"Is he capable of having Thayer beaten to cover up?" I said. "Or doing it himself?"

Hedger scowled. "Well, yes, I suppose so. He is tough enough, as Angus says."

"I've thought and thought," MacDougall said, "and some competitor who wants an advantage on us is the only reasonable answer."

"Not very damned reasonable then," Hedger snapped. "That study won't give them much on us, and we have a hundred competitors anyway."

I said, "The key is your *decision*, right? What you decide to do on the basis of the report from Stanniger. That would be valuable."

"All right," Hedger agreed. "That would be worthwhile. But we won't think of a decision for weeks."

"How about if Jon Calvin was working with someone inside your company? He gets the report, it's studied, and then an inside man listens and watches for signs of a decision. Tyrone even suggested that."

Hedger and MacDougall looked at each other. Stanniger drummed away on his desk. MacDougall was glum, and Hedger was silent for a time. MacDougall found his voice first.

"Tyrone suggested that? He's a shrewd man. Something like that might work without the inside man actually being in on the decision."

"Tyrone is shrewd," Hedger said, "but not that stupid. It's a possibility, I admit it, but it's not reason enough. The risk isn't worth the candle. There must be some other, more urgent reason behind it all."

"Okay," I said. "You people tell me. I'm on the outside. Why did you hire the study in the first place? Who was in on the whole thing? MacDougall said he was against it?"

Hedger began to pace. MacDougall's big hands twisted together. It seemed to be a habit when he was disturbed.

Maybe he was thinking about Jon Calvin. Or Eric Calvin? Max Stanniger sat watchful.

"The entire management team considered the matter," Hedger said. "As you know, we're planning a new, quality line. It's an expensive venture. We've always had our market surveys and forecasts made inside, but lately we've been wrong a few times. The market is changing rapidly. Two of our younger vice-presidents, DiBello and Cooper, suggested that Stanniger do the poll for us. Angus considered it a waste of time and money, and I tended to agree with Angus. DiBello and Cooper took it to the Board. With the unrest over Vietnam, the riots, inflation, the Board decided the survey would be useful."

"You were outvoted?"

"The matter was hardly of great importance."

"Why did MacDougall oppose it?"

"Because we don't need it," MacDougall said, angry. "We can do our own damned thinking and studying. I've analyzed the consumer market for years. I'm not sure we can even trust Stanniger, and if that's offensive, I'm sorry."

Stanniger gave no reaction. I had a hunch he had faced the same kind of opposition from older executives before. It was a hazard of his business, and he wasn't a man who took offense if there wasn't money in it.

Hedger said, "The report was only one small factor in our planning. We'll study it, Angus will make his report, I'll give my analysis, and everyone will present a case before we act at all. The only question now is what happened to the study, and why? What about that girl Angus mentioned to me?"

"She knew Jon Calvin," I said, "and she's vanished."

"Well, there!" Hedger said. "Why would she vanish if she wasn't implicated?"

"You both know she's Ben Mills's daughter?"

"Of course," MacDougall said.

Hedger didn't know. "Assemblyman Mills? You mean he may be involved? He can't be trusted out of sight!"

"Can you think of any specific reason he'd want the survey? For himself, or for someone else?"

"No," Hedger said. "Nothing specific. No one ever knows what Ben Mills might be up to."

"None of you can tell me anything definite?"

MacDougall looked at the others. Hedger shook his head.

# THE FALLING MAN

Stanniger raised negative eyebrows. His face implied that it was my problem—he was paying for it to be my problem.

"Someone beat Thayer, and planted that microfilm," I said. "Someone who doesn't want anyone looking around, and who seems to know what's going on."

Stanniger said, "Perhaps Thayer can tell us something soon."

"Thayer can tell us nothing," I said. "The man who beat Thayer did it to stop him looking, not to stop him talking. He could have killed Thayer. He's not a man who kills if he doesn't think he has to, but if Thayer had known anything he'd be dead."

Hedger and MacDougall were shaken. Violence was not part of their normal lives. They dealt each day with problems that could cause pain, violence, even death, but they never saw that part. They saw impersonal, abstract dealings. But they were also the kind of local tigers Norman had described when they were threatened, and one, or both, of them could be acting.

"Thayer may still die, be dead already" I said. "I don't give much of a damn about your study now, except that I'm counting on it to lead me to Thayer's attacker. I'm going to get him."

I left them watching each other, but seeing little except their own thoughts.

# 29

AT THE HOSPITAL they said that Thayer was still alive. He had been four hours in surgery, was now in Intensive Care.

"When can I see him?"

"We should know more in a few hours. If you'll excuse me."

I stood in the corridor. We need to look at a sick person to be sure he is alive. Hospitals have the feel of death, and deep inside us is the magical belief that all will be well if we can see and touch. There is a fear that out of sight is to be already dead.

I went out into the darkening street. Night comes early and fast in upstate New York in November. I was tight, in knots. I needed an hour alone, and a drink. First a shower, then some drinks—alone—to think.

I pulled away from the curb. The other car came away behind me.

A big car. A Lincoln. The driver was alone as far as I could see in my mirror. I made a sharp left into the quieter side streets of New Park. The Lincoln turned after me. I did twists through the side streets to be sure. The Lincoln stayed with me, not trying very hard to seem innocent.

I slowed twice, passed more than one deserted spot. The Lincoln came up each time I slowed, but fell back. He took no advantage of the deserted places. Then I made a right, and the Lincoln vanished.

I was puzzled—until I found no way to turn off the road I had taken. It ended back at the highway, and the Lincoln was there. He knew the town. I speeded up and drove to my motel. The Lincoln parked at the motel behind me. I slipped out my pistol, and walked back. I held the gun in plain sight.

# THE FALLING MAN    113

Angus MacDougall had his alert eyes on the gun as he stepped from the Lincoln.

"I have to talk to you," he said.

"What about?"

"Can we go inside?"

I stepped around a car parked near my unit, and unlocked the door. He nodded to me in that automatic gesture of the boss accepting the politeness of his inferiors, and went in first. He began to talk before he was a full step into the room.

"I can't . . ."

He stopped. The sound, noise, from his throat was something strangled.

Crouched, my gun out in both hands to shoot wherever my body aimed it, I saw what had stopped him.

"Is he . . . ?" MacDougall croaked.

Walter Tyrone sat in a straight chair. He was not going to get up. His chin rested on his chest. His arms hung loose, the hands limp, boneless. His feet were splayed out at grotesque angles with no relation to each other.

"Call the manager," I said. "Over there, the telephone. Tell him to get the police. Make him check the time."

MacDougall could not stop looking at Tyrone. There was a time when all men lived with death, but no more. Now the average man could live most of his life without meeting death at close range, and MacDougall walked toward the telephone as if not sure where the floor was.

I looked around the room. It was empty and undisturbed. There had been no struggle. The bathroom door was open, and so was the rear door. My bag had not been touched. I went to the open back door. It had not been picked. It had an ordinary spring lock, and had been opened with a key. Not the regular key because I had that in my pocket.

Outside the rear door there was nothing to see. Like most country motels, all the elegance was in the front facing the highway. Behind the units was uncut brush, hard ground, and trees. A man with a car would have been out and in his car within seconds, leaving no trace on the rough, hard ground.

The bearded manager came through the front door. He was the calm type. He looked at Tyrone as if he saw dead men every day. Then he looked at me and at MacDougall.

I said, "We came in together," I looked at my watch, "about four minutes ago. Right, MacDougall?"

"Yes," he said. "Together."

I was an outsider, a snooper, and I had talked to Walter Tyrone not long ago. Without MacDougall I'd have been up to my neck in mud. I needed MacDougall.

"We touched nothing. We didn't touch the body. Right, MacDougall?"

"Yes, right."

"You got that?" I said to the manager.

"I got it," he said.

"Did you see or hear anything near this unit?" I asked.

"Not a thing, mister. It's the last unit. I was in the office watching TV. Cars come and go, who looks?"

I stood over the body of Walter Tyrone, my eyes taking in everything. He wore the same suit he had earlier. Nothing was torn. One of his hands had a long scratch on the back, but I could see that there was no skin or hair under his nails. From marks on the rug, and from the fact that there was no sign of any struggle, I guessed that he had been killed in the chair.

I raised his head by the hair. I had to force my hand against repugnant muscles that didn't want to touch him. It's a reflex. Death must be unknown, untouched.

His eyes bulged, his tongue protruded from a gaping mouth. He had been garroted from behind while seated in the chair. The killer had stood braced, had pinned Tyrone to the chair by the force of the cord around his neck. It didn't take long, and the body was warm. Dead between ten minutes and a half an hour.

I went out front. Police sirens wailed in the distance. The hood of Tyrone's car was hot. I looked inside, on the floor, in the glove compartment. There was nothing. I went back into my unit. MacDougall sat on the bed now. The second reaction had set in for MacDougall: his face was turned rigidly away from the dead man.

The manager went out to wait for the police. I lighted a cigarette, and was aware of the manager standing where he could watch both the road and us inside. I spoke low.

"You had something to tell me, MacDougall?"

He licked his dry lips. He seemed to feel the weight of gathering forces that filled the room: the insistent presence of the dead man; the police sirens growling closer; my grim voice; his own chaotic brain. Like a man in a vortex.

"Yes," he said. "I had an idea. About Stanniger."

"Stanniger?"

"What if he sold our report to a competitor, perhaps more than one. He became afraid we'd learn, so he hired Jon to steal the report and provide a reason for the data leaking out."

"Then hired us to catch Calvin?"

His voice was stubborn. "He had to make the theft look real. He was confident you would find nothing. Overconfident."

"No," I said. "There wouldn't be enough money in that to make Calvin risk jail. The competitors wouldn't have stood still for being labelled thieves after buying the data. They'd have spilled it all. Too much risk, for too little."

He let that sink in. The sirens were closer now. The bearded manager outside still had one eye on the road, and one eye on us through the open door.

"All right," MacDougall insisted, "I've long had the suspicion that consultants like Stanniger use their studies to influence the stock market, and make a bundle. There would be a lot of money in that."

"How would it work?"

"Stanniger gives the data to some brokers. They leak it to big investors, hold it back from small ones, and manipulate the market. No real theft, so no buyer to be found."

"We find Calvin to prove there was a theft, but we don't find where the report went because it went nowhere?"

"Exactly. Jon and the theft was a ruse to protect Stanniger if the market began to act oddly. He can say the report was stolen, but no one knows where it went."

It was the best theory so far. I had found no real trace of a buyer, the film had been in Calvin's room, and there might be enough money in it to pay Calvin to take a short prison term in silence. Jon could easily have invented some tale about not seeing who paid him. Stanniger had been ready to call it quits with the finding of the film, let it end at Calvin.

I was still thinking about it when the police sirens growled into the motel lot. MacDougall got off the bed like a puppet on a string. Captain Katona of the New Park police came in with the bearded manager telling him the story. Katona sort of came to attention when he saw MacDougall.

The gray-haired Coroner was behind him. Sam Norman

brought up the rear. Norman looked at the dead Tyrone, at MacDougall, and at me. He did not seem to like what he saw.

Captain Katona didn't like it, either. With a respectful nod to MacDougall, he gave me the full cop stare: "Let's hear your story, Shaw."

# 30

MACDOUGALL WAS ALL that saved me from at least a long night in the lock-up, being sweated hard.

"You got a lot of luck," Sam Norman said.

The police had gone, Tyrone's body had been carted out, and only Norman, MacDougall, and I were left in the motel room that was uneasily dominated by the empty chair where Tyrone had died.

"MacDougall wanted to talk about Stanniger," I said.

The Coroner had confirmed my guess: Tyrone had been dead no less than ten minutes, no more than half an hour, when I had found him. With the hospital people, and MacDougall, to testify, I was clear. So was MacDougall, and just about no one else.

"What about Stanniger?" Norman said.

MacDougall repeated his suspicions. He sounded less sure now that he was telling them to Norman. The Wayne Center cop thought them over for a time.

"Possible, I guess," he said at last. "He had time to get here after you two left his office, if he don't have an alibi. So did Mr. Hedger. Katona'll check out all the alibis."

"The manager said a man tried to call me twice in the last two hours," I said. "I thought Tyrone knew something when I was with him. He must have decided to tell me. He couldn't reach me, so he drove down. The killer spotted him. Tyrone must have known the killer. The killer opened the back door, told Tyrone he'd found it open, got him inside, and killed him. Tyrone trusted someone too far."

"Maybe Ben Mills or that Levine punk," Norman said. "Eric Calvin called me to tell you he got something new about Miranda Mills and Jon. I was on my way down when I picked up Katona's radio call."

"What new information?"

"He wouldn't tell me, except he says it ties Jon and the girl close to the whole thing."

"All right," I said, "but what I'd like to know is how the killer knew Tyrone was coming here."

"Tailed him," Norman guessed. "Or had you staked out here."

"Unless Tyrone told him he was coming to me. Whatever Tyrone knew, he could have told me earlier. Maybe he wanted to warn the killer he was going to talk, give him a chance. You said it's all a club up here."

"I said it," Norman said. "So everyone better be careful who they talk to. He's getting jumpier, it looks like."

MacDougall stood up. "If there's nothing more we can do now, I'll go home. My wife isn't well."

"Tell us if you think of anything else," I said.

His feet crunched through the gravel outside, and his car door opened and closed. The motor faded away, and the motel room became silent. I remembered that drink I had needed what seemed like ten hours ago. I picked up the telephone.

"What do you drink?" I asked Norman.

"You name it."

The manager could get me a bottle, with ice and mixer. I ordered Scotch, with some soda. I hung up to wait. Norman was staring at the empty chair where Tyrone had died. His rough hands rubbed across his eyes. His lips skinned back.

"Lice," he said. "Old women. Too rotten to do it like the law says, and too yellow to take real chances."

His voice was high with rage. I wondered when my bottle would come. It looked like he needed a drink, too. He stood, and began to walk in violent strides.

"Killers, all of them! Every day they kill people they never see face to face, and when they slip and get caught they cry. Ruin you when your back's turned, all legal and safe. You seen them, Shaw, you know. The respectable men. The whole lousy world kills people every day. The easy way. Not the hard way and take it win or lose, no, not them. It's a stinking world."

Tyrone's murder had gotten to him. His neutral cop's eyes

had the anger in them far down. He stood in the room for a full minute longer. Breathing hard. Then he walked out.

His car started, crunched gravel, faded away. I sat alone. Ten minutes later, when my bottle came, the violence of his anger still filled the room.

# 31

I SAT IN darkness with my whisky and a growing anger of my own. I had two stiff drinks.

Where was the crime?

The crime big enough to have made Jon Calvin so desperate? I had been attacked, Cassandra's apartment had been bugged, Thayer had been beaten, Tyrone had been murdered, Miranda was missing. All to cover a crime, but what crime? Where was the crime in the beginning to have started it all?

A two-bit report had been stolen. A slap-on-the-wrist crime. But after that Jon Calvin lured Miranda to New York and tried to kill her. He failed, came to search my office, and I killed him. I spotted Miranda, lost her, and . . .

Then it got serious. My unseen shadow appeared.

That first night, after I lost Miranda, but before I knew anything, or had even started to try to find out who Jon Calvin had been, and what he had wanted with me.

I put down my glass in the dark room. I had been attacked before I ever got to Jon Calvin or Miranda, but after I had seen Miranda on the street. So my shadow had seen me try to catch Miranda, and he had been already waiting at Cassandra Kingsley's place. He had been hovering around *Miranda!*

I identified Jon Calvin, talked to Miranda, and then Miranda vanished. Cassandra Kingsley vanished. Thayer was beaten up here; after Miranda vanished, but before Cassandra did. I came up, found Thayer, and Tyrone was murdered coming to talk to me.

I stood up, paced the dark room, and hit the wall with my fist. Where was the crime?!

Nothing but a petty theft, I was sure of it. How had it changed, and when? I couldn't put my mind on it, but I sensed that somehow after Jon Calvin had fallen from my

# THE FALLING MAN

window it had all changed. I had the feeling of seeing a tiny hole in a dike grow, suddenly, into a violent, runaway flood.

I sat down, poured another drink, and started to go over it again.

The steps in the gravel outside my door were quick and light. I put down my glass and reached for my pistol.

There was a soft knocking. Not knocking at all, more like someone scratching quietly. I waited. The scratching came again, insistent. I stepped to the door and jerked it open.

Dr. Cassandra Kingsley stood there. "Hello, Paul."

She came in. Her lips smiled, but her eyes were wary. She watched me; tall in a long, brown leather coat. She didn't ask why I was sitting alone in a dark room.

I put the gun on a table, put my arms around her as tight as I could, and I kissed her. She didn't pull away. She met me more than half way. Her body was all muscle, and all, somehow, soft.

# 32

THERE ARE TIMES when you're so sure you can let the moment wait. So sure that you can see it all clear and be uncertain. She wanted me, Doc Cassandra, as much as I wanted her. That's the best feeling a man can have. But it makes the end important, and then you have to face the end, the reality. It's not just an adventure anymore.

"For ten years I worked to be what I wanted, ruthlessly," she said, her lips on my cheek. "For five years I've been who I want to be. We can decide."

"Do I fit?"

"I'm not sure. I think you could. I know I want you."

"Then there's no hurry. A drink?"

"Yes. I need it."

We were on the bed. Her coat was off, nothing more. She was long and slim in the same green slacks but a different blouse—a dark red blouse with a high neck. I didn't see any parts of her now, only her, complete. I went to pour the drinks. She sat up against the headboard. I gave her a drink, and sat in a chair facing her. I didn't turn on the lights. How long we would wait I didn't know yet.

"I went to find Miranda," she said. "I thought about what you said, about whether she was a victim or part of some crime. If she was involved, I didn't want you to find her first."

"Did you find her?"

"Not a trace. I drove all over the city, out on the Island, to Connecticut. I went to all her friends I know. I contacted every Digger apartment. I have ways of finding someone like Miranda, people who will talk to me. She's not in New York. She hasn't gone to friends unless she came up here to the camp."

"Levine says she didn't. A gas station man on the Thruway near New Park thinks he might have seen her about an hour and a half after she left your place."

"You think Jerry's hiding her?"

"Maybe."

"What did her father say?"

"He doesn't know anything, and he doesn't want to."

Her calm eyes glinted at me in the dark room. She leaned her head back against the headboard, her eyes closed. Her throat was long and pale and alive. "We're a loving people, aren't we? A loving, understanding species. All of us. The only species on earth that habitually preys on itself, hates. Miranda can't love him, either."

"Gray isn't a fashionable color," I said.

"No. Black and white, like me."

"Are we going to be black and white, Cassandra?"

She smiled in the dark. "I don't know. Perhaps we should be, but we'll probably be gray all the way."

"Do we find out?"

"How long will you be here? Do you still want to find Miranda?"

"If I can. Have you been to the camp?"

"No. You mentioned a man named Stanniger. I called him as soon as I got here. He told me where you were."

I told her all that had happened. I watched her as I told it. I wanted her, and I had to trust her, but all I knew was that she said she had been looking all day for Miranda. Her long, slim body shivered once, and seemed to draw in on itself on the bed in the dark. She drank, looked at the room.

"Here? In this room? Murder?"

"Yes," I said.

"And your partner," she said. She drank again, held the glass against her face. "It's your work. Why?"

"My wife asks that, too. I tell her it's what I do. I don't know any better answer. Maybe it's to help the Jon Calvins in time, help the Mirandas. Who asks why he does what he does as long as he finds something in it?"

"I do, Paul."

My glass was empty. I got up and filled it. I took her glass and refreshed her drink. She watched me with those calm, sure eyes. I sat down again. I was facing the chair Tyrone had died in.

"Eight years ago I wanted to be an actor, maybe a playwright. We worked hard, Maureen and I. She had the talent. We needed money. I became a detective. Every time I walk around the Village all the eager kids could be Maureen and me eight years ago, except that it's not eight years ago. Maureen is a fine actress now, the eagerness has changed into art, and art has limits, discipline.

"I'm a detective, and that has discipline and limits. I know what I can and can't do. When I see those kids I think of what Conrad said: 'I remember my youth and the feeling that will never come back—the feeling that I could last forever, outlast the sea, the earth, all men.' I'm only thirty, but I lost that feeling in Vietnam, and I'm a detective who likes his work most of the time."

"The detective and the fallen professor," Cassandra said.

She didn't seem to expect any answer or comment, so I said nothing. We sat with our drinks and listened to the night, the cars on the highway, the voices from the other units. She was a woman who could sit content in silence. I smoked my cigarette all the way, and half finished my new drink.

"Why?" she said. "Why all of it, Paul? What could Miranda know about murders, beatings? The way she described that boy, Jon Calvin, how does he fit into such things?"

"I don't know," I said, "but Miranda is in it."

"I'll go to the camp, talk to Jerry. He has to know something."

"When will you go?"

"Tomorrow? Yes?"

"You're sure, Cassie?"

"No, damn you, I'm not sure. In fact I'm damned unsure. I know what we want, but what do we need?"

Before I could answer that big question, a car drove into the motel lot and came to a hard stop outside the unit. A big car. I could feel it directly in front where Tyrone's car had been. I got my pistol. Cassandra sat quietly.

The car door opened. Feet crunched gravel. I went to the door. The knocking was loud, insistent.

"Shaw? Let me in. Ben Mills."

I opened the door from behind it, looked through the space between door and frame. He was alone and empty-handed. I stepped around the door. He saw the gun. His coarse face showed no expression, his nervous mouth set in a hard line.

He came in. "Did you find Miranda?"

"No." I closed the door, and held the gun.

"I heard about your partner and Tyrone."

I put on a light. "Where were you this evening?"

"You mean for Tyrone? I never touched him. I was out looking for Miranda, but I never came near here."

"Looking where for Miranda? You said you knew nowhere."

"Okay, I lied. I know some old friends, some hangouts, but she wasn't . . ." He saw Cassandra. "Who's she? I want to talk alone."

"A friend of Miranda's. She knows all about it."

I got a flash of how Mills worked and triumphed in his slick world.

"So?" he said, "Miranda has beautiful friends."

As smooth and warm as soothing oil. He adapted like quicksilver, changed in an instant according to who he was with.

"What did you come for, Mills?" I said.

His gallant expression fell like an elevator. He had a mind made up of a thousand small compartments, each totally separate, and he changed from one to the other at the pull of some switch inside him.

"I'm scared," he said, like a beaten dog. He had been acting so long he could not turn it off if he wanted to. "She's my daughter, no matter what kind of life she lives."

Cassandra said, coldly, "What kind of life is that, Mr. Mills?"

He sat down and looked at Cassandra. The beaten dog fell away leaving some pose I did not recognize at once. He took out one of his cigars, bit it, spat, lighted it.

"Okay, miss," he said. "I know what you think is right, and what you think of me. Okay, I got morals, and that's funny. Morals from Ben Mills. That's the way it is."

I realized why I had not recognized his new pose—he was being real, honest. It was probably the first uncalculated moment he'd had for years.

"You weren't scared earlier," I said. "No worry at all."

He chewed the cigar. "You said she was mixed up with this Jon Calvin. He's dead. She's missing. Maybe she's dead, too."

"What makes you think that?"

I was thinking of Jon Calvin trying to kill Miranda. He heard it in my voice.

"Tell me," he said. "She's my girl, Shaw. My kid!"

"Jon Calvin tried to kill her in New York, but that's all I know."

"Calvin?" he said, his thick face really surprised. "I don't get it. I thought maybe the other guy, but why Calvin?"

"What other guy?"

"He came to me this afternoon. A bum! Long hair, mustache, dirty clothes. Said he had to know where Miranda was."

Cassandra said, "Jerry Levine?"

"That's him. He was pretty wild, so I told him to get out, and then he told me."

"Told you what?"

"They're married. Him and Miranda," Mills said. "You know, my mother was Italian. I grew up with Italians. You got any idea what it means to an Italian father when his daughter gets married? And I wasn't at the wedding. I didn't even know she was married."

"You're sure?"

"He showed me the certificate. Said he guessed I wouldn't want to believe him. Over a year they've been married."

"And he came to you looking for her?"

His thick, smooth-operator's face was aging before my eyes. Haunted by sudden fears. "You think he's covering up? If she was playing with this Jon Calvin, he wouldn't have liked that, right? Maybe she was running out on him. Maybe he stopped her? He knows where she is, he put her there, and just came to me to look good?"

It was a cold thought. Jerry Levine did have a lot of violence in him. He hadn't told me they were married, or anyone else as far as I knew. I turned to ask Cassandra if she'd known. I looked around the room. Cassandra was gone. The door was open. Outside a small car started up and pulled out of the motel lot.

"Shaw?" Mills said. "Is she dead? He killed her?"

I barely heard him. I cursed him under my breath. All of them, the whole damned case! Cassandra was gone. There was no hurry for us, but today was gone, and today never came again.

"Shaw? What do you think?"

"Nothing. I don't know. Levine's a strange man."

"Yeh," Mills said. "You know, when I asked around about Jon Calvin, I got to like the sound of him. Not Levine. I don't like him. How do you understand a man like Levine? What does he want? Jon Calvin I understand. A hungry kid. I know about hungry kids. They go places, get things done."

"Levine has a different hunger," I said.

I was trying to think of what the marriage meant. Jerry Levine had gone to New York, looked for her, tailed Eric Calvin and MacDougall. A free agent, Levine had said she was, but did he consider a wife a free agent?

"You know," Mills said, "if they're right, that Levine and Miranda, my whole life is nothing. Zero. This new world they want, it makes all I've done, all I got, a big zero. I've done nothing except get old and feed my face good."

"You don't have to believe them."

"But do I call them bums, phonies, just because if I admit they could be right, then all I've done doesn't amount to a hill of beans?" Mills said. "Do I hate them because I've got to believe my life was important?"

"You'll have to answer that yourself," I said.

He nodded vaguely to that, and started to look around for his overcoat. He realized he had come without a coat. He stood up, looked confused. Unless he was a complete faker. Or maybe just himself—a man with a thousand narrow little rooms in his mind that never connected to each other.

"You don't have an alibi for Tyrone," I said. "Do you have one for my partner? Last night about midnight?"

"I was alone except for Trevino."

"Which doesn't count. Maybe you were in New York the last few days? You or maybe Trevino?"

"She's my daughter, Shaw."

"From what I hear you love a shady deal as much as you love Miranda, maybe more. The two problems could be separate."

He almost smiled. "You make a man feel at home, you know? You've got a mind as lousy as mine. Find Miranda, I'll pay you a bonus, then get off my back!"

He went out walking taller, back in his element. I got my bottle. Before I finished my first drink, wondering if I should chase after Cassandra and knowing I shouldn't, the telephone rang. It was the hospital. Thayer was going to make it. It would take time, but he'd live.

There was a lot I could do. Go to Eric Calvin and find out what news he had for me. Check back on Tyrone. See what the police had learned about the alibis for the time of Tyrone's death. I finished the bottle instead. To hell with the case.

# 33

I WOKE UP with a sense of loss, a feeling of guilt, and a hangover. I had a cigarette. Then I took a long shower—very hot and very cold—and dressed. That helped the hangover.

The feeling of guilt would pass once I got to work. I couldn't do much about the sense of loss: last night was gone. I holstered my pistol, and went out for breakfast. I had missed dinner, so I ate a lot. I thought about Cassandra. I told myself she had wanted to talk to Jerry Levine, nothing more.

I didn't want to think about Maureen. I didn't want to have to think about Maureen, not now. I wanted to float in a limbo—the case, myself, and Cassandra. I had forgotten to call Maureen. Too busy to call, of course. If I didn't call, I didn't have to think. But I had to call her. I finished my coffee and found the telephone. Maureen was not at the hotel. I left a message. I never call her at a theater. It was a reprieve. I went to my car and headed up for Kingston and Eric Calvin's address.

It was a small house on a dead-end street that backed on a miniature swamp. There was one level on the street, and a lower level that opened onto a backyard and the swamp.

A tall, gray and white-haired woman answered. "Yes?"

"My name is Shaw, Mrs. Calvin. Paul Shaw."

I didn't have to say more. The name Paul Shaw lived in this house. Two tears showed in each blue eye. The memory of her loss was close under her surface like a fish beneath very thin ice.

"I'll call Mr. Calvin," she said.

She forgot to ask me in, but that was all she did after the tears. I stepped in and closed the door. Eric Calvin appeared in the narrow entrance hall from below. In the days that had passed his grief had hardened into anger. He glared at me.

Stood and glared. His wife appeared again behind him. She touched a reddened, veined hand to his shoulder. She was as tall as he was.

"Eric," she said.

"I know," he said. "We called for you, Shaw. Come on down."

I went downstairs with them to a sunny, large room that faced the backyard and the little swamp through picture windows. It was a homemade room. Probably Eric Calvin's pride. I could picture him working weekends, and after work in summer, year after year to make this room with its view like a miniature estate. The boy, Jon, had probably helped him. But Jon was gone, and the swamp was frozen in winter cold.

Nobody sat down. Calvin looked out at the view for a moment. "Jon used to make believe this was a castle when he was a little kid. The swamp was a moat. He rode out like one of them old knights. 'Sallying' he called it. Couple of years ago we went up to see the Vanderbilt place near Hyde Park. Jon said it wasn't so different from my big room, only bigger. He said we'd all have a place like that someday."

"Jon had a fine home, Eric," Mrs. Calvin said.

Eric Calvin shrugged. He had taught his son right. What had happened?

"You had some new information, Mr. Calvin?" I said.

"Yeh," Eric Calvin said. "It's worse now, eh? I heard about Walt Tyrone. It don't make much sense."

"We're sorry about Mr. Thayer," Mrs. Calvin said.

"Thanks," I said. I didn't say that Thayer would live. I didn't want to hurt them more. "What is your information?"

Eric Calvin turned from the window. "Jon and that girl was closer than we thought. Too close. Maybe they was in on something together, and maybe it wasn't all her. They was going off together."

"Is it true that she's pregnant? Sergeant Norman told us."

"Yes," I said. "You think that maybe they planned the theft together, intended to run off with the money?"

"Yeh, it looks like it. Only you . . . Jon got killed. She still missing?"

"Yes."

"Yeh, she said she didn't want to live."

"But with a baby coming?" Mrs. Calvin said.

# THE FALLING MAN

I said, "Where are you getting all this?"

Mrs. Calvin opened a drawer in a bureau in the room and handed me a sheet of paper. It had been folded to fit an envelope. It was a letter, typed, unsigned:

*My darling Jonny,*
*Last night, and all our nights, are the world to me. I can still feel you beside me as I write this in my bed. I want you with me—always. If anything went wrong I couldn't live without you. But nothing will go wrong. The people I know will pay a lot, and no one will ever know. Then we can live our lives far from here. Do you miss me as I miss you? I know you do, I feel it each night we're together. Come to me soon.*

*All my Love,*
*Miranda*

It was cheap bond paper that could be bought anywhere. There was no envelope.

"Where did you find it?" I asked.

"In Jon's desk, among some papers," Mrs. Calvin said.

"When?"

"Yesterday afternoon."

"You hadn't been through his desk before?"

"Yes, I had, but I must have overlooked it."

"Were there other letters like it? From Miranda?"

"No."

"You must have seen his mail. Did he get other letters that could have been from Miranda, or any girl?"

"Not that I remember, no."

Eric Calvin said, "It was her idea, you see? She says she knows people who'll pay a lot. The way she says it I figure those people wasn't from up here. New York, maybe."

"Yes," I said, "that's what someone wants us to figure."

Mrs. Calvin heard me, and understood. Maybe she had known it had to be a fake all along. Eric Calvin didn't hear me. He was still finding people who had led his Jon astray.

"Those people, outsiders," he said, "they must be the ones running around killing to cover up."

"The letter's a fake, Mr. Calvin," I said. "It has to be."

"Fake?" he said.

"Pretty crude, too. It's typed and unsigned. It doesn't even sound like Miranda. It wasn't here until yesterday, and there are no others like it. If Miranda had written to Jon, it would have been to his New Park room. It's too obvious."

"But why, Mr. Shaw?" Mrs. Calvin said. "How does it help anyone?"

"Mr. Calvin already spotted one way—it suggests that Jon was working with outsiders. It says Jon and Miranda were in it together, and it maybe gives a reason for Miranda to be missing. Not bad for one little letter. It fits with some other things, too. A note in Jon's room blatantly tried to implicate Walter Tyrone. A roll of microfilm was put back in Jon's room after it had been searched. There was a sloppy try at hiding where my partner was attacked first."

I looked at the letter. The typewriter might be traced, but I'd have to have some hint where to look first. "Someone is trying to confuse the mess, send us off in all directions, not frame anyone special. Playing for time, maybe."

Eric Calvin said, "You mean that letter was planted here?"

I nodded. "Who's been in the house the last day or so?"

Mrs. Calvin sighed. "Almost everyone, Mr. Shaw. They all came to offer their sympathy. Some of them people we didn't even know, but who had known Jon."

"MacDougall and Hedger?"

"Most of the brass from the company," Eric Calvin said, not without pride. "We got good men up top."

"Stanniger?"

"Yes," Mrs. Calvin said, "and that Sergeant Norman. We really don't know either of them. They all liked Jon, you see."

I didn't tell her that Stanniger and Norman couldn't have cared less about Jon. If they had come, it was at best a duty call, probably pushed by MacDougall. Unless they had had their own reasons?

Eric Calvin said, "Ben Mills and that creep of his come asking about Jon. There's two I don't turn my back on."

"Some strange young man, too," Mrs. Calvin said. "Levine."

"Him I tossed out on his dirty nose," Eric Calvin said.

Everyone, which wasn't much help. I said, "Who was close to Jon the last few months down in New Park?"

Mrs. Calvin thought. "His adviser, perhaps. That's some Professor De Lange down there."

"Thanks," I said.

"When will they let us bury him, Mr. Shaw?" Mrs. Calvin said.

"They ought to clear up the red tape in New York soon, Mrs. Calvin."

In my car I lighted a cigarette, and thought about that phony letter, and about Eric Calvin. Mills had been right; I had a lousy mind. Perhaps that's why I like being a detective. I work, day in and day out, with the worst in men. It makes it easier to face the world without surprise.

Eric Calvin would have had a better chance to plant that letter than anyone else. If he had been involved in it at all with Jon, he had no reason not to protect himself now. Jon couldn't be hurt more. Eric Calvin had insisted all along that Miranda was the cause of it all, and now the letter seemed to confirm that.

The letter also did something else—it prepared for a dead Miranda. The hint of suicide. A voice in the back of my mind had been telling me for some time that Miranda was dead. It had been too long. I had not wanted to hear that voice inside me. Now I had to hear.

# 34

PROFESSOR HERBERT DE LANGE was a jovial little man who sported a red vest under a hunter-green blazer. His eyes twinkled as he waved me to a seat. It was the only chair in his office not piled with books and papers.

"Jon Calvin? A bright boy, but lazy."

"Lazy?" I said. "That's not the picture I have. Summer work, football, ROTC, always busy."

De Lange nodded. "True, a hard worker in that sense. Lazy was the wrong word. Mentally lazy. No, not that. What do I say? 'Soul' lazy? Yes, exactly that. A quick student, but never a complete job. Sloppy work, no depth. Facile, not thorough. Jon never worked to learn, but to get the marks. Class status, you see? Short cuts to triumph."

I remembered Jon Calvin's books in his New Park room. Self-help manuals, the glories of the successful and the tricks of the trade, the secrets of how the "lucky" made it. Schemes and romantic inspiration.

"Did you have any idea of some real shortcut he might have had in mind? Some important event about to happen?"

"For Jon everything was of great import. A boy who thought in superlatives, grandiose."

"Something immediate, real."

"Nothing I knew."

"What about girls? Did he talk about girls?"

"Jon? No, that wasn't one of his hang-ups. Not Jon."

I described Miranda—her appearance, her ideas, her life. De Lange's eyes went up all the way. He began to shake his head.

"If Jon was hanging around that camp, and a girl like that, it was for a quick make, perhaps for his amusement. He would have considered those children as specimens, not people. He would have thought of such girls as tramps, promiscuous. The common notion. He would have had no idea what they were really after, could never have understood a girl like that."

"Would he have stolen, Professor?"

"Absolutely not, no."

"But he did. We have proof. There's no doubt."

"For money? I don't believe that."

"For something else, then."

He considered. "Who can say? For an opportunity, perhaps. Some dazzling opportunity to gain success, position. For that Jon would have done almost anything."

"A shortcut?" I said, as much to myself as to De Lange.

"For a good shortcut to high places, yes," he said. He leaned back. "Jon is dead? Killed in some kind of accident?"

"Yes, an accident connected to the robbery."

"When would the robbery have been?"

"About a week ago, probably. Last Wednesday or Thursday."

De Lange frowned. "On Friday last I did notice something. He came to morning class, but he was, well, distracted. He hurried away. On Saturday he did not appear at a special session."

"He was killed on Saturday night," I said.

Perhaps it was the naming of a concrete day he could place in his mind, but as I left he seemed suddenly depressed. He sat smaller, looked out his one window to the campus where he tried each day to teach boys like Jon Calvin about life.

# 35

A GREEN MG sportscar was parked in front of Jerry Levine's cabin at the camp when I walked across the creek on the footbridge. There were no other cars in sight, and no one moved at the camp. I heard no sounds of work or music. The crazy-patch but solid cabins hung on their hillside deserted in the sun. The only movement was a thin pillar of smoke rising from the smokehouse.

Cassandra met me at the door of Levine's house. Her calm, mature eyes told me that she, too, had lost last night and was sad.

"I'm sorry, Paul. I felt so secure, I didn't think of us."

"I know," I said. "I thought of us, later."

"I had to talk to Jerry. It's true. He's worried."

We went inside. Jerry Levine was at his workbench. He looked even more like some Biblical prophet in a long poncho made from a blanket. His deep eyes were sunken. His hands worked on his shoes. The work was his security.

"He'll talk to you now," Cassandra said. "You will, Jerry?"

Levine's hands went on with their work. Deft, automatic, separate from his brain. "I don't know. It's a long time since I tried to communicate, Doc."

He put down his shoe, and studied his hands. They had the same permanent dirt ingrained in the creases that Eric Calvin's hands had. "You know about Red Cloud, Shaw?"

"The Sioux chief?"

"Almost the last." He picked up the shoe again. He needed his hands busy. "When he gave up the fight against us, he made a speech to his people. A scornful speech, ironic. He told them, 'You must begin anew and put away the wisdom of your fathers. You must lay up food and forget the

# THE FALLING MAN 137

hungry. When your house is built, your storeroom filled, then look around for a neighbor whom you can take advantage of and seize all he has. That is the way to get rich like a white man.'"

He hammered two nails viciously. "Most people believe that what their world tells them is true, is not only true, but is the only natural way for men to live. The Indians lived a different way, by a different truth. So there's nothing natural about our society, nothing that is human nature."

"So?" I said.

"So we here see a different way. That makes most people hate us. We don't have any connection to your robbery, or your violence, but no one'll believe us. That's why I wouldn't talk to you. To mix in it at all would just get us attacked."

"Not if you weren't really involved."

He shrugged. "It wouldn't matter. Some Greek said it, 'A man can escape every danger, but he can never escape those who just don't want such a person as he is to exist.'"

Cassandra said, "Demosthenes. He was too right."

"But now you'll talk to me?" I said. "For Miranda?"

He began to cut out a sole from thick leather. "I don't know why Miranda's in trouble. She wasn't having any affair with Jon Calvin. We mean a lot to each other, we want our life, we have our kid coming. She was just his excuse for coming up here. He had his eye on some of the single girls. Guys like Calvin always think our girls are easy."

"Why did she meet him in New York, Jerry?"

"She told you, didn't she? She thought maybe she could help him. She saw him as confused, driven. That's why she sort of took him under her wing here, and talked to him a lot down at Stanniger's."

"She's that dedicated to her ideas?"

"You know what 'community' means to us? It means nobody is bad or outside. We've got a commitment to everyone, if we like them or not. Miranda believes in 'community,' and if Calvin needed her help, then she had to help him."

"And you? She's your wife."

"What does that change? We got married, legally, just so we didn't give the law an excuse for bothering us. All of us get married for that, to keep the 'good' people from hanging us. Words on paper don't make a marriage."

"Then why not say you were married?"

"First, because it's no one's business. Second, because we may be nuts, but we're not fools. If I told you, or the law and squares like that Sergeant Norman, you'd figure I had to be jealous, out to get Calvin, maybe to kill Miranda. You'd see Miranda as dirty, and me as burning up."

He hit me pretty close to home—what else had I thought? The obvious, the classical triangle. Like everyone else.

"You weren't jealous, Jerry?"

"Jealousy comes from ownership, Shaw. I don't own Miranda. Okay, I'm no saint. You don't change what you were born into that easily. I didn't like Calvin, I didn't want Miranda to go to New York. I went to find her, I looked around, I watched your office a while for her, and I tailed that MacDougall and old man Calvin. But that was all after, you understand? I did that when she didn't come home Saturday night. I'm not hung up on my own fears, and Miranda's a free person. Only she decides what she has to do."

"But you went to Ben Mills, to Jon Calvin's parents."

He finally pushed his shoes and tools away. "I'd decided she was just working something out. She has the right. Then you showed up here. I got worried, and I looked around. Now Doc Cassie says you talked to a gas station guy who maybe saw Miranda on Monday night near here. If she got that close, she'd have come home."

"You're sure, Jerry?"

"She'd have come home, no matter what. Good or bad."

"What are you going to do?"

"We already told the police; they're looking. All the kids here are out looking, too. New Park isn't so big. We'll find her. If she came up here, and didn't come home, she's not hiding on her own, but we'll find her."

I let that sink in. The deserted camp had the unearthly feel of a ghost town. Buildings, paths, owned by the sound of the wind. In my mind I saw all the long-haired, bearded, booted young people combing the streets, the roads, the hills for one of their own. Their isolated world invaded by an insidious outside world they had fought so hard to escape. But there was more in Jerry Levine's words than a vision of alienated youth dragged back into a society they rejected. There was the answer to my big question.

"The crime," I said. "A crime big enough to explain the beating and killing to hide it. Kidnapping."

"Kidnapped?" Levine said. "Miranda?"

"Kidnapped," I said, "maybe killed. I'm sorry, Jerry."

"Why? Why kidnap Miranda?" Cassandra said.

"Because she's a danger. She knows something."

"She said she didn't know anything, Paul," Cassandra said. "If she's been kidnapped, then she wasn't part of the theft, and she had no reason to lie. Why didn't she tell us what she knows?"

"I don't think Miranda is aware of what she knows," I said. "It couldn't be that she saw Jon steal the poll, that she'd have remembered. But it's something that someone else thinks is very dangerous. Not Jon Calvin, probably the buyer of the report. He kidnapped Miranda."

"Because she knows something about a minor robbery?" Jerry Levine said. "He turned that into a kidnapping?"

He was right. The kidnapping looked like a hell of a stupid move. Yet what else explained all that had been done since? Nothing I could think of, and yet the kidnapping looked bad. Jon Calvin, with a big chance in his grasp, had motive to kill Miranda if he could get away with it. But the buyer had no such strong motive. He hadn't even done the stealing. If he did think he had to silence Miranda, why not just kill her in New York? Had he taken her from New York so he could kill her in some deserted place? Risk being seen with her just for that?

We sat in the homemade cabin for what must have been fifteen minutes, saying nothing. The letdown. With kidnapping in mind, I would start all over again, but for these immediate moments I felt I didn't have the energy to move. Miranda's clothes hung on their rack, abandoned. I was staring at them when the silence slowly changed into the sound of a motor on the dirt road. A truck. It throbbed up to the camp, and someone came running across the footbridge. The door was flung open.

The youth in buckskin I had met the first time I had come to the camp, Berger, came in.

"We found this, Jerry," he said.

He held up the Egyptian Key of Life amulet that was like the one Levine wore, and the one Miranda had worn. Levine took it, turned it over.

"It's Miranda's," Levine said. "Where was it?"

"A side-road off the highway from New Park to here. It was right where the road meets the highway. There's a couple of houses near the highway. We asked. One old guy says he heard a car drive fast up the road last Monday night around eleven-fifteen P.M. He was watching the news on TV. A small car, he says, with a motor sounded like a sewing machine."

"Volkswagen," I said.

Berger nodded. "That's what I think. We called the fuzz, Jerry. They must be up there by now."

"Fuzz? Cops? Up where?" Levine said.

Berger couldn't look at Levine. "Jerry, there isn't anything else up that road after those first houses except Moon Lake. You know Moon Lake, Jerry? It's got almost no bottom."

Levine went out the door like a blind bull going into the bull ring. Berger just did reach the truck before Levine drove off. I dragged Cassandra to my car.

# 36

THE NEW PARK Police were there, and the State Troopers. When they have a job they know, like dragging a lake, the police move with skill and speed. Captain Katona was at the edge of a high bluff where the dirt road ended above the lake.

"My wife," Levine said, his eyes fixed toward the smooth water below that shined in the winter afternoon sun.

"We don't know she's there," Katona said. "Go and sit somewhere. You, too, Shaw."

Cassandra led Jerry Levine away. He was in a trance. I didn't leave. I had seen lakes dragged before, and rivers, and sometimes it has to be done through the night, and then it's a grim scene with the boats out on the water moving back and forth, the skin-divers shivering on shore before it's time for them to go back under, the dark vehicles, the glaring lights, the knots of silent people.

This wasn't like that. Moon Lake was small and placid with a sense of silent depth. Its steep shores were heavily wooded with green pines, and it shined in the winter sun like a postcard scene from some resort. The small boats dragging the edge looked like fishermen on a holiday. The skin-divers were like small boys sporting. Even the people, all troopers and police and the kids from the camp, looked like vacationers. There were no houses around the lake—state land.

"Why drag only the edge?" I asked Katona.

"Too deep. If we don't find anything we'll have to send for suit divers. Maybe that won't be any good."

"What makes you think she's in there?"

Katona nodded to his left. The marks of the narrow tires were obvious. They went right over the edge of the bluff. Only the glass-smooth and ominous lake was below.

"You want to hear what ties in, Captain?" I said.

He nodded. He didn't like all that was going on, but there was no way for him to escape it. I told him all I knew, or guessed, so far. I didn't elaborate on the problems.

"Is that all of it?" he asked.

"You've got a killer around here, Captain."

"That make you feel good?"

"I'll feel good when he's caught."

"That's nice for you."

I walked away. He had his work to do, and he'd do it, but I knew what was on his mind. He could know the killer.

I followed back along the Volkswagen tracks. I found nothing. Cassandra and Berger sat with Jerry Levine on a grassy patch. Levine slumped with his head hanging down. If Miranda was in the lake, Levine had lost much more than a Calvin because of her beliefs. Jon Calvin had taken advantage of those beliefs, whether he knew it or not.

I found the patch of oil in dry grass some fifty feet from where the Volkswagen looked like it had gone over. A small pool of motor oil in a clump of dogwood hidden by a grove of pines. It was a slow leak, a car had been parked there for some time. The tracks it had made leaving along the dirt road were over the VW marks in places.

"What do you think it means?" a voice said.

He was a chunky man in a brown suit. The suit was neat and neutral, neither cheap nor expensive, and the man himself was neat and neutral. A face no one would look at twice: bland and mild—except for a pair of shrewd eyes, and a set to his mouth that indicated both world-experience and authority.

"A car was waiting here," I said. "It left after the VW went into the lake, if it did. It doesn't look like there were any other cars beyond the two. It might be connected to the VW, it might not be."

"You think it is, right, Shaw?" he said, and said, "I'm McCann. Inspector McCann, State Police."

"I think it is, Inspector," I said.

"Why?"

"Because it's set up to look like suicide, and it wasn't. No one could drive up that dirt road and go off the bluff by accident. So either someone was with her and drove her over, or someone with her sent the car over empty, and then used the second car to get away—with or without her."

# THE FALLING MAN 143

"Or she drove it over empty herself, and got away in the second car," Inspector McCann said.

He wasn't Captain Katona. He was a detective, not a rural cop, and murder was a prime concern to him.

"I don't buy that," I said. "She's a victim, not a conspirator. She didn't vanish and drive here, she was kidnapped and forced to drive here."

"By the same man killed Tyrone and beat your partner?"

"I'd say so."

"And it's tied in with the theft of that report?"

"You've been working on it," I said.

He smiled. "I've been around. Since your partner was found. Any ideas?"

"Some," I said. He'd been around, and I hadn't run into him. A quiet, efficient worker.

"I'm in the dark," he said. "I don't know enough, about this Mills girl especially. I'd appreciate . . ."

He got no further. A call floated up from far below in the cold lake. We both hurried to the edge where Captain Katona was down on his knees leaning over the edge of the bluff. Below, one of the rowboats had snagged an object. Cassandra, Jerry Levine and Berger were at the edge now. Levine was being held back as if he was ready to plunge off the bluff to find her himself.

"Take a look!" Katona shouted down.

As we all stood there in the winter sun a skin-diver took his air hose into his mouth and dove. All the other boats stopped their work to watch. On the high bluff no one spoke. On the lake a loon laughed insanely, and dove, as if it, too, wanted to see what was down there.

The diver surfaced, removed his mouthpiece, shouted up: "It's there!"

*. . . there . . . there . . . there . . .* echoed across the lake.

"Empty!"

*. . . ty . . . ty . . . ty . . .* from the wooded hills.

Katona bawled down, "Any sign of her?"

"No! Windows and doors open!"

Katona waved his arms. "Look! All of you!"

The divers went out and down. Jerry Levine sat on the grass at the edge of the bluff. Cassandra spoke low to him. The divers and boats worked in a widening circle.

"She could have floated anywhere," Katona said.

"She'd have floated up," McCann said.

"Unless she stuck under a ledge, a rock, trees," Katona said. "That bottom's rugged, and the lake's so deep we might never find her. She wouldn't be the first in Moon Lake."

The name of the lake sank into my brain. All at once. Moon Lake. It gave me the answer to why someone had turned a minor crime into a kidnapping. Like that. I was sure.

"Moon Lake," I said. "Where they found that gambler who could have testified against Ben Mills?"

Katona said, "What are you talking about, Shaw?"

"That gambler," Inspector McCann said. "Sure. Are you saying Mills tried it again? His own daughter?"

"Sam Norman told me," I said.

"Maybe Mills faked this?" McCann said. "To help his daughter hide out?"

I didn't have enough to say anymore. But I was sure of the reason for the kidnapping. Someone had been playing for time all along, needed time. The reason for Miranda's kidnapping was the same as for most kidnappings—ransom. There were two men behind it all now, not one. The man who had hired Jon Calvin to steal the report, and a second man who was the one who had kidnapped Miranda. A second man who had been watching Miranda from the start, who knew how dangerous she was to the buyer of the report Calvin had stolen.

Katona said, "We better see if we can find her before we start making guesses about who pushed her in."

"You won't find her," I said.

"You're sure?" Inspector McCann said.

"As sure as anyone can be without proof."

"That's not sure enough," Katona said. "We can't stop looking on your hunch, Shaw."

He was right. No police force could stop looking for a body on my hunch. He turned his back on me, and began to give orders to call for suit-divers, more skin-divers, and equipment to raise the Volkswagen.

McCann said, "Can you give it to me, Shaw?"

"I can't guess for an Inspector in front of witnesses. I could be wrong. But find Sam Norman. Ask him about Moon Lake."

# THE FALLING MAN

I went to my car. Jerry Levine was on his feet beside Cassandra. He held to her arm like a drowning man.

"Paul?" Cassandra said.

"I'll be back," I said.

I had no proof, less than half of the story, and I didn't want the police moving too soon. I didn't want to give Levine too much hope, either. I was sure Miranda wasn't in the lake—not yet. But I could be wrong. It was all a matter of time.

If she wasn't in the lake, she would be soon. I might be too late even if she wasn't dead yet. Because if I was right, she was being held for a new kind of ransom—a ransom that would be paid not to free her, but to be sure she was killed.

# 37

THE SUN WAS low when I reached New Park. All I had to go on was my new hunch that there were two men, and the conclusion I had reached last night—that the second man had been following Miranda in New York. Not Jon Calvin, or Thayer, or me, or anyone else—not at first. He had gone to New York after Miranda.

There were two clerks at the ticket windows of the New Park bus station. They looked tired, and it was not yet five o'clock: the day-men. I got on the shorter line. It inched forward, but my turn came.

"Were you on duty Saturday?" I asked.

"I'm always on duty, mister. Where to?"

"I'm looking for a man," I said.

I showed him my license. He was more than a little afraid, but he was an ordinary man, he wanted to help. "What man, mister? We get thousands."

I described Sam Norman. "He would have been asking questions like I am. About a passenger who had taken the bus. About what bus she'd taken."

He didn't recognize my description. The second clerk did:

"Sure, I remember him."

I switched windows. "On Saturday?"

"Yeh. It was after my lunch break. I'd been for some beers. I always go to the tavern on Saturday to watch the football. It was Saturday."

"And you remember him? How?"

"Easy. He was tall and skinny and like a cop. They can't hide it, being a cop. He had a side arm under his slicker. A cowboy kind of hat. He asked questions. I remember."

"Who did he ask about?"

"A girl. Showed me a picture. Snapshot, kind of fuzzy,

# THE FALLING MAN 147

but a nice-looking girl. Funny clothes. I sold her a ticket, too. She had a serape like, red and black. I been to Mexico."

"What did the man do?"

"Bought a ticket for New York, too."

I went out of there. I felt just a little fogged in the brain. So easy. Such a careless mistake for a man like Sam Norman to make. Except it hadn't been so easy—five days of work, a lot of walking and talking, and even more hard thinking and good guessing. It only looked easy—now.

I drove north for Wayne Center.

The sun blinded me low in the west, and I thought about Sam Norman's mistake. It had not been so careless. Almost inevitable. Five days ago what had he had to hide? There was no crime in following a girl, and who was going to ask about it anyway? He had probably done nothing then, had just been hired to follow Miranda. He hadn't known then what he was going to do later.

When he had first known, I couldn't say, but he had been careful to make sure that Lt. Baxter and I thought he had come to New York on Sunday to look for Jon Calvin. Eric Calvin had asked him to find Jon, of course, but that had been only a cover. If I was right, Norman already knew that Jon was dead when he agreed to look for him.

The sun was gone when I reached Wayne Center. I sweated under my clothes as I walked into police headquarters, but I tried to keep my face calm. If I had to accuse Sam Norman of kidnapping and murder in his own town, police headquarters was the best place I could think of. They wouldn't believe me, but they would have to listen, and Norman couldn't use his gun or his garrot here. He would have to tell them to go ahead and investigate him, and make his run for it later. With any luck, I'd be in a safe place by then.

I didn't have the luck.

"Sergeant Norman isn't here, Shaw. Off duty."

"You know where he is?"

"Kingston. Something to clear up over there, he said."

"Kingston police?"

"That's right. His old buddies," the desk man sneered.

His voice told me that Sam Norman had a way of flaunting his city experience. I didn't care about that. What I cared about was looking for Sam Norman in the open. I could just tell my suspicions to the Wayne Center police, take the chance I was right. That was the safest way in the long run. But there was still the third man, and there was Miranda. I risked Miranda that way. They would give Norman every break, aware of it or not, and Norman had killed already—if I was right.

I drove to Kingston. It was fully dark now. A cold night with a menace of snow.

# 38

LT. CESARE DALIO, Kingston Police detective, considered me across the desk in his dim night office.

"Sam was here, you missed him by about fifteen minutes," Dalio said. "I could put a call on the radio. He usually tunes in police calls wherever he is."

"No," I said. I said it fast, and Dalio noticed that. "Do you know where he went?"

"No. He got a phone call, and went off."

"A call? From where? Who?"

Dalio shrugged. "I couldn't say. What do you want with Sam, Mr. Shaw?"

"Is he a good friend of yours, Lieutenant?"

"I've known him twenty years, we worked together for ten years," Dalio said.

"That's not what I asked."

"We're friends. As much as anyone is Sam Norman's friend. He's in trouble, Shaw?"

I lighted a cigarette. "What do I say? He's a cop, so are you. You worked together. I'm following a hunch and my nose. How are you going to take it?"

"It's the Stanniger thing? Walter Tyrone?"

"Yes."

"From what I hear, that Jon Calvin lifted the report and sold it to someone. Sam Norman wouldn't buy it, so if Calvin stole it, where does Sam fit in?"

I smoked, listened, and saw a glaring fact in the way he was talking. "You're not surprised he might be in trouble?"

"He's all law, and always has been. A hard law man. He never broke a law in his life, or bent one."

"Maybe he never had a good chance," I said.

He let that float around loose in the dry heat of his office.

He didn't agree with me, but he didn't disagree, either. He was a fellow cop, something of a friend, but he knew things about Sam Norman that made him sit there in silence.

"Why did Norman leave the Kingston force, Lieutenant?"

Dalio chewed on that for a time. I waited. There is a sense of timelessness, of suspension from reality, in all offices of policemen. A detached, isolated world.

Dalio said, "He started on the Syracuse force. He was married then, had two kids. His wife remarried some kind of accountant. Sam used to talk about that: how she walked out on him and couldn't do any better than a four-eyed pencil pusher who didn't even know how to spit and still never made a buck. The kids are grown up. He used to send them money."

"Why did the wife leave him?"

"He always said she didn't have what it took to be a cop's wife. He talked about her a lot; too much. He still does. Her and his kids."

"You think she left him for another reason?"

Dalio squirmed. "Look, I said Sam was all law, a hard man down the line. To Sam, if a man breaks the law, and gets caught, he should expect to get punished. A man should admit it's right he gets punished. Sam always hated anyone who wouldn't take his punishment."

"Like Ben Mills?"

"Yeh, like Ben Mills. Sam hates anyone who lives by wits and tricks, sharp deals. A real man to Sam keeps the law hard, or breaks it hard and takes his chances. The only criminal I ever heard him say a good word for was a bank robber who busted jail just to kill his wife's new lover, then holed up on top of a mountain and held out four days before the cops got him with a sniper rifle from five hundred yards. Men he hated most were guys he said wanted to live without making any enemies."

"You think his wife was afraid of him?"

"Maybe," Dalio said. "Sam's one of those guys always riding off on the edge, carrying a whip, and it's all a war. We had to let him go because he had to be too hard, prove he was better than any man, especially any businessman gone a shade wrong. Wayne Center likes their cops hard, and they like Sam. All that doesn't say he's a killer."

"Would he kill for money? A lot of money?"

"You tell me, Shaw. Sam could do most anything he decided had to be done. I don't know about money. He was sometimes bitter about never making much because he wouldn't play the tricky games, but he isn't the kind of man who ever needed money much."

"But he would kill?"

Dalio watched a wall. "Sam never gave a damn about getting killed, and it never bothered him to have to kill another guy. It's all man-to-man with Sam. Only I don't hear anything yet from you says Sam killed anyone. You got any real proof?"

"I'll get the proof, and I hope it's not another killing. Will you hold him if he comes back?"

"You making an official charge?"

"If I have to."

"Then we'll hold him. But that's all, you got it? So far all I hear is a hunch. Sam Norman's a rough man, but he's always been straight. No one up here's going to work against him on what you've got so far."

Dalio was a cop, and no cop wants to accept the thought that another cop has gone wrong. He would hold Norman, but that was all he would do, or could do. For more positive action, I was on my own.

The night had grown colder with a cutting wind as I drove back to Wayne Center.

# 39

NORMAN WAS NOT at Wayne Center Headquarters. I hadn't really expected him to be.

The telephone call to him had been some kind of warning, I had no illusions about that. Probably from the other man in the picture. Who, or how, I didn't know, but I had no doubt that Norman knew he was on a slippery edge, and I was not going to find him in a nice, safe police station.

I got his home address, and drove out of the little town. I didn't expect to find him at home either, but I had to start somewhere to find a lead to where he was. Miranda's life could be hanging on minutes, if she wasn't dead already. I had to hope he had been caught short, and had to move fast without time to cover his tracks. I had to hope I would find some clue at his house to lead me on the right trail to Miranda.

The blacktop country road had little traffic in the night, and I drove fast. There was no more need for caution, for hiding the fact that I was looking for him. Norman wasn't a man who would pack up and run without a fight. For all I knew, Miranda was dead, and he was down at Moon Lake brazening it out, challenging fate to prove what he had done. He would make us, me, prove he was guilty of anything. He would make me come to him. And I had to go. I couldn't give him time. That would end Miranda for sure. My only hope was to charge around in the open, press him so hard that he couldn't risk killing her for fear I would pop up at any moment to catch him.

The narrow, dark road led me west and south toward the mountains that were hidden in the night—only a darker mass in a dark sky. I drove thinking of how I would approach his house. A lot depended on what I found when I got there. I had my gun, but he had his, too, and he would be a better shot. I didn't think he would be there, but you never knew with a man like Norman. He might even have Miranda there, it was the kind of bold play he would make. I would have to try to get close unseen, take him at a disadvantage before he knew I was there.

I almost laughed in my own face at that one. I wasn't the man to take Sam Norman at a disadvantage when he was alert for danger. No man was. Expose myself, and trust to luck. I wasn't going to trick him, I was going to have to beat him.

I swung into a curve, came over a small rise in the road, and the car pulled across the road ahead of me.

I had no chance to stop.

The car moved out of the trees to block the right lane just below the rise. I was almost on it. The road was dark, empty, whipped by a cross-wind.

I tapped my brake, gripped the wheel hard, braced for the shots I was sure would come, and steered into the clear left lane.

No shots came.

In the left lane I was past the car, already turning back for the right lane, when I saw I couldn't make it.

Just beyond the car that blocked me, at the bottom of the small rise in the road, the road took another sharp curve to the right. I couldn't turn fast enough without flipping over. I had to go off the road to the left.

There were trees, a shallow ditch, and a hill going up. I went off the road, fighting to brake and slow, dodging the trees. My mind told me, calmly and logically, that it was a very nice trap. I analyzed, clearly, that the spot had been picked with care, with complete knowledge of the road, and of the capabilities of modern automobiles.

I missed two trees, lurched through the shallow ditch, swayed out of it half sideways, came down to 30 M.P.H., bounced off a small tree, and hit the upslope of the hill. The grade slowed my car down to 20 M.P.H., I was feeling almost elated, when the car met a big, bare oak head on. It stopped with a shudder, and flip up of the rear, and my head cracked full into the windshield.

Groggy, I tried to move. I had hit at 20 M.P.H., was only dazed, and knew by some urgent instinct that I had to get out, move and run. I couldn't move. I tried again. I lurched in some direction. I wasn't sure which way I was going. I had the door open. I heard the quick footsteps. I sensed the other car, close. I thought, very clearly, that I had come to a stop at an almost exactly calculated spot. The other car had followed me. Very neat.

Something hit me.

# 40

TOO LONG. NO one stays unconscious so long unless he is dead.

I saw my wristwatch through some weightless, waving, undulant sheet of plastic. 3:12. Darkness and a hanging light. So 3:12 A.M. Of what day didn't matter. At least eight hours. No one unconscious from a blow to the head that long can be alive.

"You sleep nice, Shaw."

He sat across a bare wood table. There was a coffee pot. A pot for boiling coffee, battered. A mug. Two plates with the remains of something.

"Relax," Sam Norman said. "The time don't matter."

He smoked, tilted back in a straight wooden chair, the pale Stetson on his head. Tall and whiplike, in the hard black suit made for work. The hat low on his brow. Small-eyed, his thin lips working the cigarette around for taste. Pistol in his belt.

"Eight hours," I said, croaked in some strange voice I had never heard. I looked for who had spoken.

"I got you juiced up. You're okay. A tap with a billy, some needles. You're bruised up some."

"Drugs?" It was my voice, croak. I thought it was.

"Couldn't leave you on the road. Too close to my place. When'd you figure me for sure?"

"Moon Lake," I croaked. "Where . . . Miranda?"

"Worry about yourself." He rubbed at his lean jaw. "Moon Lake, huh? Hell, how careful can a man be?"

The sheet of plastic began to undulate between us again. I said, "What . . . what happens . . . now?"

"We'll figure out something."

I gathered my strength and dove for his throat. Hurled myself across the bare table. My fingers groped through the thick plastic air for his throat. He slipped away like a ghost; a mirage; some ancient demon; the Devil himself. He flowed like liquid through my fingers; a mocking miasma, his thin face melting into a dark, black pool . . .

5:32.

My watch read 5:32. Clear and steady. The sensation of undulant plastic was gone. There was a faint gray haze of light outside the windows of the cabin.

It was a cabin. There were four walls, furniture, a stove, a refrigerator. I saw two windows and an outside door. Two inner doors to other rooms. Outside there was the rustle of large trees. I heard no sounds of traffic, no voices.

Norman still sat tilted back in the chair across the bare table. The hanging light was still on. He was reading a book, smoking. Two hours, more, since I had dived at his throat. Except that I had not dived. I had not moved, I was tied, neck to feet, to a chair. The dive had been all an hallucination, the drugs. I had passed out again. Now the drugs had worn off.

"It's over," I said. "You can't kill us. They found the Volkswagen, and they know I was looking for you."

He didn't look up. "I'll work it out."

"They'll look for me."

"Not for a while. Who knows what a detective is doing, right? No one looks before maybe noon. You were chasing a wild hunch, you were wrong, there's no proof." He put his book aside, looked at me from under the brim of the Stetson. "Too bad you got into this, Shaw. I got no reason to go against you. A bad play all around for both of us."

"Kidnapping, murder, assault? A real bad play. You can't make it now. And just for money? In the end, just money?"

He shrugged in the chair, chewed his cigarette.

"No," I said, "not just money, not for you. The challenge, the chance to beat the world, prove you're a better man. It was there, right, the opportunity, and you had to take it to show what a man you are? The dare? A daring raid you just couldn't refuse."

We talk with our hands. Did you ever try to talk seriously with your hands tied behind your back? It feels all wrong. You can't make your words strong enough. "Jon Calvin stole the report for someone. Miranda knew. Calvin got worried. So did the someone who hired him. The man who hired

Calvin then got you to watch Miranda, paid you. You tailed her to New York."

"I did, huh?"

"I checked the New Park bus station."

"You're a pretty good detective. I guess I should have stopped you."

"Were you hired to kill her, Norman?"

"I'm no hired gun!" He glared at me from under the Stetson, his deacon's face outraged. "Anyway, my pigeon ain't got the guts to hire a killing right out like that."

"Who is he, Norman?"

He laughed. "The gold goose, Shaw. The scared bird's gonna lay me a nice egg."

"So you just watched her?"

"See she stays quiet, scare her off. You know the play: bad morals, frame a charge, plant some dope on her."

"But you didn't?"

"No chance. Calvin messed it with that dumb act in the park."

"You were in the park?"

He laughed again. "I was supposed to find out what you guys knew, too. I'd spotted Thayer 'cause he reported to the New Park cops. After the girl run off in the park, I figured it was a good trick to send the kid to your office. He jumped at it, the jerk. He'd stripped like a spy, see. He already had that mask—some dumb idea he'd wear it to make his getaway from the park. I slipped him the old gun and the keys, and he run off like in seventh heaven. One hungry kid."

He thought for a moment, lighted a new cigarette. "I guess I should of gone myself. Me you wouldn't have knocked out any window. Only you did me a kind of favor killing the kid. That kind of changed it all."

His voice was objective, dispassionate—I had done him a favor killing Jon Calvin. The dawn was full outside now, but he didn't care about the dawn. A man alone on an empty planet.

Where was Miranda? I could only talk, wait. Norman was right, they would not miss me for a long time. "You lost Miranda when I did, so you tailed me, listened at my door. You staked out Cassandra Kingsley's place, and garroted me Sunday. I caught you in the hall, and you didn't want anyone to get even a glimpse of you. You decided to have a reason for nosing around, so came back here and got Eric Calvin to send you after Jon. You must have missed Miranda here Sunday, and went back to New York to find her. You tried the Emerson, she might have gone there to try to learn what Jon had wanted with her. When you didn't find her anywhere, you must have decided to watch me in case she came to me with what she knew. When I found the Emerson you knew the clerk would tell you'd been there, so you showed up to convince Baxter and me that it was Jon you were after. After the morgue, when you still couldn't find Miranda, you came back here again, and you found her at the camp."

He had lapsed into a watchful silence as I talked. His eyes were barely visible under the Stetson brim. Steady eyes, his deacon's face neutral, detached, listening.

I talked. "You planted your car at Moon Lake, rented or borrowed another car, and planned to snatch her up here. You didn't get a chance, and tailed her back to New York. You must have been nervous when I got to her first. Your scheme depended on her not telling what she knew. You already had the apartment bugged, earlier, and you found out Miranda didn't know what she was supposed to know. That was perfect. You waited, called me to be sure I was out of the way, and when she came out alone you took her. You made her drive up here, sank the Volkswagen, and hid her. You held her for ransom. If you get paid, you silence her for good. If you don't get paid, you turn her loose to tell what she knows—making sure she really knows what to tell."

His chair hit the cabin floor with a bang as he leaned toward me. His voice rasped now. "Not bad. I saw the chance when the kid did his dive, thanks to you. That put my man in real deep. I had him cold. A chance like that don't come along too much. If anyone knows my man even tried to get that report, he's ruined. He don't want anyone knowing he got the kid killed. Then I mixed him in a kidnapping! My pigeon."

"You mixed him in assault and murder, too," I said. "Why did you beat Thayer?"

Norman swore. "That damned Tyrone called my pigeon on Monday night. Tyrone wanted my pigeon to get Thayer to lay off him. My pigeon told me about Tyrone calling. I didn't want Thayer nosing around while I was waiting for the payoff.

So I figured what he was up to at Tyrone's, and went and tapped him."

"So that's what Tyrone had to tell me? When I talked to him, told him when Thayer had been beaten, he remembered the call he'd made to your man, and put it together."

Norman shrugged. "You can't cover it all. Tyrone made a big mistake. After you left him, he called my pigeon again to say he had to tell you about the Monday night call. My pigeon was scared witless, and called me. If you heard what Tyrone had to say, you'd sweat my man and he'd break. So I tailed Tyrone to the motel and got him."

I shivered. The cuts and bruises from the car crash had begun to burn and ache, but that wasn't why I shivered. Norman had "got" Tyrone. Like that. Not a monster, Norman, no. In my mind I saw him in my motel that night, raging at the world. Tyrone's killing had gotten to him. Death and guilt had reached him that night in the room with the empty chair, and he had raged at the world in hatred of his own guilt. The world was bloody, and guilty, because he was, so he had raged. But he would kill again if he had to, and I didn't have to ask what would have happened if I had been there with Tyrone.

"Now you collect?" I said.

"Soon. My pigeon had to sell stocks on the quiet."

"He won't pay. You can't talk. It cuts both ways."

"He don't know I won't hang us both. He's gutless. Anyway, I can still ruin him with the girl."

"You can't turn Miranda loose."

"How you figure that?"

"She knows you now."

His deacon's face twisted in disgust. He was annoyed with me. "She don't know me. My pigeon's dumb, but not that dumb. To make it all work from the start, I had to make him know I could turn the girl loose without fingering myself, right?"

He kicked his chair back, and stood up, in one fluid motion. There was muscle in his whip-like body. He ambled to a rough chest and took out a large sack with eyeholes cut in it. "This comes down to my shoulders. I wore me a big coat. I didn't talk. I hid in back of the car. She don't know me at all."

He dropped the sack back into the chest. "I can turn her

loose anytime to finish him. He talks about me, he hangs himself."

"Too much risk, Norman."

"Everything got some risk. With luck, she talks, he's ruined, the rest goes in the Unsolved File. No one knows about me."

"I know about you."

He just looked at me across that dawn room. He didn't say anything. The silence spoke for him. I tried to think of a flaw. If Miranda didn't know who he was, he could turn her loose to talk, and his pigeon couldn't talk back without crucifying himself. It was risky, but Norman was a man who took risks, even enjoyed the risks. All he had to do was get rid of me in some safe way. The police might even guess, but they'd prove nothing without the pigeon's help. A man who hired a robbery, then was going to let Norman murder Miranda to cover, was not going to jail, or even losing what he wanted to protect, just to make the truth come out. The pigeon was in too deep, and he might as well pay to save what he had wanted to save from the start.

Norman said, "There's two hundred fifty thousand dollars in the pie, Shaw. Come in for one hundred thousand. I kill you, it's more chance. With you in with me, everything's easy. You steer them away from me. You say you spotted outside killers like I wrote in that note I planted at Calvin's house."

"I already said that was a fake letter."

"You changed your mind, new evidence. Tyrone was in on it. Thayer had evidence. It fits, they'll buy it. Tyrone was killed by outsiders. My pigeon stays mum, we're home free."

"Miranda?" I said.

"She got to go. Hell, what is she? A tramp. A crazy anarchist no good to anyone. We do the country a favor."

"She's a lot to Jerry Levine," I said, "and to me."

His voice cracked at the edge of sanity. "She goes, damn you, if you come in or not! You don't save her hide."

"I'm not part of killing her. No."

"For her?" He stood over me. "For the truth, maybe? There ain't no truth in this world except what a man can beat out of the world for himself. You gonna die for truth, Shaw? For her? Maybe for my pigeon? You figure you can save my pigeon? A big man thinks no one else counts? A yellow liar got to hire that report stolen to make himself look good? You figure to die for that?"

I said, "What are you, Norman? An animal?"

"A man, mister. A man never had a dime, and now I'm gonna have a whole lot of dimes. Sam Norman, Shaw, all alone. I'll laugh rich."

"A crazy animal," I said. "Crazy."

His fist moved two feet. I went over in the chair, my jaw numb and stabbing pain at the same time, and skidded into a wall. I lay helpless. All I could move were my eyes. I saw him over me.

He kicked me in the head. In the chest. He kicked . . . kicked . . . kicked . . .

# 41

IT CRAWLED. BLACK. Big, and black, with six stiff jointed black legs. Ten legs. Eight. Across a streak of sunlight to my eyes. Quivering antennae. Jaws like horns. Eye to eye. Reared up. Crawled out of my sight, onto my face.

I screamed.

*Norman said, "The kid getting killed kind of changed it all." He said that, Norman, laughing at me: "You did me a favor, all right. The kid getting killed like that messed my pigeon up good." So the pigeon didn't want anyone to know he had been the one who led Jon to his death, not ever. A favor to Norman, killing Jon Calvin. Because it made everything worse for the man who had paid Jon Calvin to steal, had hired Sam Norman to protect him. Jon Calvin's death was, somehow, dangerous to the "big" man's position. It had started the change from a penny-ante crime into a nightmare. All right, that was clear. Why?*

I crawled. Through long, endless bright streaks of sunlight that glowed hazy and waved through the thick plastic sheet over my eyes. I crawled, wrapped in the shimmering shell of thick plastic. Hard wood against my face; rough wood that gouged at my ear, scraped my cheek. Unable to lift my head. Crawled on my side tied in the chair through the waving, undulant streaks of sunlight toward the door ten miles away. Ten million miles to the door and outside where the air was free.

*A big man, big. "Important man thinks no one else counts." A pigeon with a position to protect. With status and power. Big man who knew Jon Calvin well enough to know his hunger, to know the depth of Jon Calvin's short-cut dreams, to know that Calvin would steal for a big chance. A man big enough to offer, guarantee, Jon Calvin a place in the sun good enough to make Jon Calvin turn desperately to murder of Miranda to keep his chance for the short-cut to glory.*

Ten miles high, the door. No chance. No way. The door would not open to the free air and the sun outside that bathed the world in light, not in shimmering streaks on a hard floor. I could neither walk nor stand, and had no hands to reach up for the door to the open air, the light. A closed, silent door. And . . . an open door. Fluid through the thick bubble of plastic around my raw, scraped face. The pain in my chest. An open door far away . . . far . . .

*Norman said, "Ruined if anyone even knows he tried get that report. Through if they know he even wanted it." A position to lose. A reputation? A business? His whole business gone if the theft is known? Or his position of influence? How? Because he was a thief? Yes, but more. More than that. Something else. A different danger than simple caught-for-theft implied in the way Norman spoke. To have it known that he had even tried to get the report, even wanted it, would finish him.*

Open door! Open! Through the viscous fluid inside which I crawled to the open door. Open! . . . Into another room, a small room without escape.

My face against the floor. Hopeless. Breathing slow pain. Only a room.

Not empty. My eyes opened so slow, so hard, and the small room was not empty. She lay on a bed, tied to the bed. Ropes I could see, and handcuffs. Asleep. Unmoving. She breathed slowly, quietly. Long black hair disordered; a blue wool skirt; black boots.

Miranda.

I crawled. Inched my bloody cheek ahead to the bed and the motionless woman. Two of us could escape! A mistake, Sam Norman! A bad mistake. Together we'll be free, we'll be free, we'll ruin you, finish you, Sam Norman! The two of us to free each other. Okay now! It was okay now!

Okay . . .

*Norman said, "Tyrone called my pigeon to get him to tell Thayer to lay off." Who would Tyrone call to make Thayer stop bothering him? A man of influence: Ben Mills? Hedger, a big man at Regent-Crown? Perhaps, perhaps, but there were three men who had hired Thayer, us, to investigate. Three men could be Thayer's bosses, Tyrone had heard.*

*MacDougall, Stanniger, Eric Calvin! Not Eric Calvin, no, not a big man, no position to lose. Stanniger with a business, and MacDougall with high status.*

She breathed slowly, a rattle in her throat. Deep sleep. Too deep. Below the bed, her long black hair above my eyes, and no way to reach her: no way. She would not wake up.

No way up to her.

Teeth were no good. Teeth did not work on hard, tight ropes. Teeth did not loosen handcuffs.

No knives, no razors, no nails so lucky, no broken glass. No miracle was there. No miracle would come. Not for me.

I crawled, sideways, the streaks of sun smaller, thinner, paler. Thin, cold wind scouring the floor. A lower sun. Too late. Too late.

*Norman said, "The kid getting killed changed it all." Norman said, "I can still finish him as a big man like all along." A big man who wanted a two-bit poll report that would be common knowledge once turned over to Regent-Crown and revealed to the Board of Directors. Norman said, "A yellow liar got to hire that report stolen to make himself look good." A useless report, no value to anyone. To look good, not be finished, hold his status, his . . . And I knew! To look good! I knew the value—the simple, stupid, ridiculous value of that stolen report!*

Thin, colorless streaks of sun. Too late. Cold crawling as I crawled. The door to air far above; far . . . far. Hopeless. Inside the collapse and the tears. I cried through the thick flowing plastic shell that squeezed me. I shouted. I cried. Tears pouring. Hopeless.

*I knew . . . I knew . . . I knew . . .*

# 42

DARK AND MOVEMENT. I opened my eyes on the same darkness broken by the solitary hanging lamp. The light over the bare table, and something moved in the cabin. Someone who moved openly, busy and purposeful—a man getting ready.

On the bare table stacks of green paper. Money. A lot of money.

My chair scraped as I tried to move.

"You don't give up," Norman said, appearing in the light, a black bag in his hand.

Nothing else moved in the cabin.

"He paid?" Not a croak now, my voice, a whisper. My throat dry and swollen thick.

"What the hell else could he do, Shaw? There ain't no other way out for him. I clean it up, and we both sit tight."

The thick plastic before my eyes was almost gone again. Something whispered in my brain . . . *I knew*. What did I know? I remembered crawling. Bright sun, thin sun, and darkness again. All day, crawling, and what did I *know?*

"She's here," I said. "Miranda. Let her go. She doesn't know what she knows."

"So you found her," he said, sat down at the bare table with its stacks of money. "You was at the door out cold when I got back. What good would it do you? You got outside, there ain't nothing. Trees and mountains, that's ail."

At the table he looked at the money for a time. He began to put the stacks into the black bag. Slowly, almost reluctant. I strained against the ropes that tied me to the chair from neck to feet. The chair rocked and scraped. He did not look up. I twisted, forced the ropes. It was useless.

"Two hundred and fifty thousand," Norman said. "A lot of money, Shaw."

"You won't use it."

"She goes into the lake. In the dark. They find her, only not for a while, and they got no way to say she ain't been in the lake all along."

"And me?"

He went on filling the bag with the money. I sat. I felt like a small boy in the hands of a giant. Outside there was still no noise, no sound of cars on some highway, no voices, no movement beyond the rustle of trees. We were alone on earth. The two of us in this cabin—the small child and the silent, ominous giant packing his money.

He packed slowly, touching each stack of bills as if he wanted to draw strength from the touch of them. Too slowly, almost stalling, prolonging the time. I heard a whimper from the next room where Miranda lay. A low, frightened whimper. He heard it, too. He seemed to listen. Then he packed the last of the money, stood up, and vanished from sight.

When he stood in front of me he held a large, jagged rock. I looked at the rock.

"Now?" I said.

"I got to get moving," he said, almost apologetically.

"An accident?" I said. "I hit my head on a rock?"

"Messy," Norman said. "I got no choice, neither. Your car runs, it's outside. They find you soon. There ain't no other way."

I stared at that rock, whispered, "You can't get away with it. No chance."

"I got to try. I got a chance. You come in with me I got a better chance. I don't like it no more'n you do."

He took a step. Stopped. Sweat poured down my face and chest. No one can die, choose death, unless the choice is his own. No one can choose to be killed without a hopeless alternative. We have few martyrs, and martyrs are men with a cause so great in their eyes they cannot choose life above it. What was my cause? Truth? It's not enough.

I stared at the rock that was to be my death. I was brave, I resisted him, refused him. Not brave, no, only the hope that lasts almost forever that I would, somehow, escape. The miracle would happen. We all believe in that miracle, it's part of our flesh—the hope that we will escape. The victims in the Nazi camps hoped, expected, were sure, as their fellows vanished into the gas chambers around them, that for them

# THE FALLING MAN

the miracle would come. They would not walk into the gas chamber, the ovens. They couldn't be killed, end, vanish forever. To the last second, as the gas rose around them. The last split instant, and I stared at the rock in Norman's hand that was my last second.

"Okay, I'll come in with you. Why not? I can use money."

I couldn't die, not even for Miranda, not here and now. I couldn't end here—now. The sweat poured down me, and I began to explain to myself. I would not join him, of course. Fool him. Live to expose him. Miranda would die anyway. I would play along with him, be cunning, destroy him even if I could not stop him from murdering Miranda. I could avenge her. Yes.

"No," Norman said. He held the rock, watched me. "You'll figure on playing along. I can't trust you now."

"The money, Norman," I said, desperate. "Once I take the money I'm part of Miranda's murder. I can't talk."

"You're scared now, Shaw. When you ain't scared, you'll turn me in first chance. You got to want the money."

Was I, at that instant, brave? Was I ready? I don't know. I want to think that I was, in the end, brave but I never will know.

I was still watching that rock in Norman's hand when the beam of a small light swept the window. A flashlight. There were footsteps:

"Norman?!"

I did not recognize the voice. Too much blood pounded in my brain as I never took my eyes from the rock in Norman's hand.

Norman swore. "Damn!"

He drew his pistol and hurried to the door. He flung it open like a man who has been interrupted in something important by some trivial incident:

"What the hell are you doing here!"

Two shots exploded the night. Norman staggered in the doorway. His own gun fired once, twice. He turned, held to the door frame, his deacon's face collapsed into a mask that was no longer human. He started back into the room.

Two more shots hammered. Norman hurled into the room, his arms jerking, his gun flying away. He smashed face down on the floor. He crawled in his blood. He lay still.

Silence.

A silence in the mountain night like a weight.

A surge of impossible joy swept through me. I think I giggled. Every nerve, muscle and fiber of my bruised body ached as the fear of death drained away. My face cracked like plaster in a reflex grin I could no more stop than I had consciously started. A grin of pure, savage delight that Norman lay dead and not me.

A grin that vanished as I heard the steps outside.

The door was still open. Beyond that door someone walked toward the cabin. It could only be Norman's big man. He could not let Miranda live—or me. Maybe he could not leave his money.

It stood on the bare table, the bag of money that mocked Norman where he lay on the bloody floor, and now mocked me where I sat helpless. My eyes were fixed toward the open door. Blood roared in my ears. I didn't hear the car motors until they broke loud and close into the silence of the room.

Headlights probed outside the door. Car doors slammed. There were voices and running feet. Shouts. Some feet ran toward the cabin. Others trampled through underbrush to the left, fading as they ran.

Inspector McCann came through the door with his pistol out. A State Trooper was behind him. The trooper kneeled down over Norman. McCann came to me.

"Okay, Shaw?"

My throat would not move. I nodded.

He had my neck and hands loose. "When we didn't find the girl in the lake, I started a search of the whole area. This cabin's only about three miles from the camp of those kids. We started wondering about you this afternoon. That Kingsley woman swore you had to be in trouble. Levine spotted your car out front about an hour ago."

The trooper said, "This one's dead, Inspector."

"Miranda," I whispered. "Next room."

The trooper went into the next room. Captain Katona came in. He glanced at me. He looked uneasy.

"Got away, damnit," Katona said. "Had a car on another road behind here."

On my feet I hung onto McCann. My legs were like brittle straw: weak and without muscles, ready to snap. I swayed and stumbled as McCann walked me around the room.

# 43

"I DON'T KNOW anything," Miranda said.

Perhaps an hour had passed. The strength slowly returned to my brittle legs. Miranda had been awake, whimpering, when they went into the next room. The Coroner had worked on her, fed her stimulants, brought her out of the fog of drugs. Jerry Levine sat with her. Cassandra held a cold compress to her head. Police were everywhere. The Coroner was working over Norman's body.

"That bastard was after something, Miranda," Jerry Levine said.

McCann said, "He was out to kill you, Miss Mills."

"I don't know why!" Miranda said.

Her wide eyes were still dazed, still frightened. She held to Jerry Levine's hand. Something had happened to her face, to her mind. It was clear in her dark eyes that were still seeing something that was not in the room; in the way she sat closed in on herself. Not fear alone, or the rejection of her beliefs, but a naked uncertainty. Her pretty face a little less innocent, a little less pure.

"Think, baby," Levine said, anger deep in his voice, hate for a dead man and a living world all over his face. "It has to be something about Calvin, that report he stole."

"Maybe a second man," I said.

"I've tried to think!" she said, her voice high and shaking. "When he kidnapped me, I tried to think what I could know. He was waiting at my car. He made me drive up here. He wore a bag on his head, a coat, and he never talked. He rode in the back, under a blanket, with a gun, and I tried to think what I could know all the way up to the lake."

"Did Calvin tell you something?" Levine pressed. "Did he say anything funny?"

"I don't remember anything."

I said, "Did you see something? He met someone, maybe."

She shook her pretty head as if it were being squeezed. "I saw Jon all the time at work, around campus, in New Park. I never noticed, you know? I mean, I never thought about him, about when I saw him, except that maybe he needed help."

"All right," McCann said, "there's no hurry. We'll put you in the hospital a few days. We'll take it easy, and go over everything you remember about the last few weeks."

"Damn you, no!" Jerry Levine said. "I'm taking her home."

Cassandra touched his shoulder. "Jerry."

"No!" Levine cried. "Your damned dead world's done enough to us! Leave us alone, all of you. Miranda just wanted to help Calvin, and you almost destroyed her. All of you. That garbage on the floor was just the tool, the Cossack for your rotten Czar-world!"

"Let her go to the hospital, Jerry," I said. "Whoever shot Norman wants her dead, too."

He was bitter, but he wasn't a fool. The color and rage drained from his Wild Bill Hickok face. He looked at Miranda. She clung to his hand. Then he nodded once, bitter but aware of the way it was, had to be. Two troopers stepped up to escort Miranda out. The Coroner stood up wiping his hands.

"Three shots, all on target. A rifle, I'd say, probably thirty-thirty. Two went through, one stuck in bone. I'll get it."

The attendants loaded Norman onto a stretcher, and the Coroner followed them out. Miranda and Levine went out with the troopers. Cassandra sat on the bare table, her long legs swinging, her calm face watching me. McCann watched me, too:

"Who?" he said.

"There was a telephone call," I said. "Norman got a call at Kingston Police Headquarters. Wednesday evening, before he grabbed me on the road. That had to be his killer."

"No," Captain Katona said. "One of my men thought you were after Ben Mills. He tipped Norman to give him an arrest."

Katona was unhappy. I understood. The telephone call to Norman that night had been made by one of Katona's men who had heard me at Moon Lake. I had talked about Ben Mills, the gambler who had died in the lake, and Sam Norman.

# THE FALLING MAN

"You can't blame him too much," Katona said stiffly. "He knew Norman pretty well. A mistake. He'll probably get fired."

"Damned near a fatal mistake—for me."

"You're okay. You want his blood?"

McCann said, "Let's talk about who killed Norman, and worry about the mistakes later."

"It has to be the man who hired Jon Calvin and Norman in the first place," I said. "Norman went for his payoff, and the pigeon followed him back here. I guess in the end he was too scared of Norman. I think he was coming for Miranda, and for me, when you showed up."

"We heard the shots up the road," Katona said. "You can thank that same dumb cop of mine, Shaw. When we started to wonder about you, he told us he'd made the call to Norman. It narrowed the search. Wayne Center remembered that Norman used a cabin around here somewhere."

"The killer's the man who wanted that report?" McCann said.

*The value of the report.* My mind said, *I knew*. What did I know? Lost in the fog of drugs.

"We never saw him, just a man running" Katona said. "He had a car on that other road. A big car."

"An important man," McCann said, "and part of the case from the start. He knew about Thayer and Shaw here."

I said, "How do you know that?"

"You told me while I was walking you around," McCann said. "You told me all about it. You said he was an important man who had to look good."

So it was in my mind somewhere. *It crawled*. A black beetle in front of my eyes. I crawled and thought. Jon Calvin's death changed it all, panicked the important man. A man ruined if anyone knew he'd even wanted the report. Not stolen, wanted. The ridiculous motive—stupid motive.

"You need rest, Paul," Cassandra said, watched me.

"Wait," I said.

"He can't run," McCann said. "Not if we'll know when he runs."

"Shut up!" I said.

Motive. The value of the report. A big man. A big car. A Lincoln? The stupid, ridiculous motive and value of the report that pointed to only . . .

I had it.

# 44

IT WAS A large house, impressive even in the darkness. Two-story, red brick, white trim that shined even in the night with flurries of early snow. A Colonial-style mansion with white columns, and all dark except for one upstairs room to the right, and faint light in one downstairs room to the left.

We parked down the road and walked up the drive. McCann sent his troopers to surround the house. The front door was not locked. McCann and I went into a large, dark entry hall. Far away, upstairs, there was distant music. A formal living room to the left was shadowed and empty. Across the living room, light showed at the bottom of a closed door. We crossed the living room to the door.

Angus MacDougall sat behind an antique desk in the aristocratic study. All the furniture was antique, muted and delicate. There were no filing cabinets, no papers on the desk, no plebian signs of work. MacDougall sat in semi-shadow with his immaculate gray-white hair catching the light of the single desk lamp. He sat stiff, reserved, one big hand resting against his left side, the other on the desk top as if posing for a Bachrach portrait. He dwarfed the small desk, as he had dwarfed desks and offices and other men all his life. A big man.

I stepped to the desk, my voice too loud in the elegant study. I could still hear the faint, distant music, and I remembered that his wife was sick.

"You hired Jon Calvin to steal the report. You wanted to know what Stanniger was going to report. You wanted to make your own report say the same. That was the reason."

He moved as if uncomfortable. His eyes flickered once toward McCann, then looked back at me. There were deep lines in his face that had not been there before.

"You made the market studies," I said. "Those two young

vice-presidents convinced the Board to hire Stanniger and bypass you. But you were going to make your own report, too, and you had to prove you were as good as Stanniger. That was a risk. Stanniger's report might be right, and your report wrong. So you got the idea—make your report identical to Stanniger's. Right or wrong, you'd look as good as Stanniger!"

He made a sound, a noise. Perhaps a groan, or perhaps a sigh. I couldn't tell. I watched the hand he had pressed to his side.

"You knew Jon Calvin's dream of shortcuts to success. You offered him the one payoff he'd do anything for—a good job; success without work or wait. It all went wrong. Jon bungled the theft. Stanniger discovered it at once and called Thayer. Then Miranda Mills learned something that would show that Jon had given the report to you."

The silence of the antique study had become unreal. McCann stood alert, not really listening, only waiting for MacDougall to make some move. My voice echoed into nothing. MacDougall breathed heavily.

"You lost your head. You told Jon there was no job if it all came out. That wasn't enough. You stood to lose all that counts most to you: position, status, respect, power. So you hired Sam Norman to silence Miranda. You knew Norman. He'd do a lot to protect a man as important as you in Wayne Center. In a way, protecting men like you was his job anyway.

"After that it was all Norman. You'd hired a man a lot tougher, stronger than you. Jon Calvin wanted your job so badly he panicked and tried to kill Miranda, and then I killed him. If it came out that you'd really gotten him killed even your old employees wouldn't talk to you. Sam Norman saw his chance. You'd gotten hold of a tiger.

"He kidnapped Miranda, and held her for ransom from you. You pay or he lets her tell what she knows and your fat world collapses. So you agreed to pay, agreed to let him kill Miranda, went along with all he did, deeper and deeper into the mud."

This time the noise, sound, was loud and clear—a deep groan. He groaned, worked his mouth around something that was like an enormous stone, and tore out the single word:

"No!"

"Yes," I said. "Miranda is alive. We'll trace the money. McCann will find the rifle you used. Your car tracks will be on that back road. If that isn't enough, that wound you're holding in your side will prove it. Maybe Norman's bullet's still in you."

His hulking figure seemed to freeze in the dim light. Then he took his hand away from his side and I saw the blood on it. I had been right, Norman had hit him. McCann stepped forward.

MacDougall's hands vanished below the desk, and came up with the rifle. His finger was on the trigger. His low voice sounded like thunder in the silent room.

"The market studies were my job. Jon worked at Stanniger's. I needed an executive assistant: fifteen thousand a year, junior executive status. He got the report, but Stanniger found out, damn him. Then that girl saw us. In my car, in a parking lot, when he gave me the film! She waved at Jon, she looked right at me. Thayer was hired. If she ever mentioned seeing me with Jon on that day, in that place, Thayer would guess the truth."

He thrashed in that delicate desk chair. "Such a small thing. A look at the report, make mine the same, hurt no one. Forty years of work, of service. What was I going to do with my life if they didn't need me, put me on the shelf? What was I without the company, my position?"

"We all get old," McCann said. "You've got money."

"Money? Did I work forty years just for money to pay for old age, to leave behind? They wanted to take it all away from me; my work, my company! A useless old man no one wants around!"

He could not see himself, see what had happened to him. He never would. A man who had come to see his own position, his status, as more important than the company he served. He was the company. What was right for him, was right for the company.

"A little thing," he said, his voice low, blood spreading on his side now that his hand no longer pressed there. "Then it was a nightmare. I . . . I couldn't stop it. Sometimes I felt I was going crazy, insane. Norman went on and on, and there was nothing I could do. I even had to pay to hire you. How could I refuse Eric when he wanted to hire you? How could I stop Norman? I had to pay him to silence the girl. I didn't know he would beat Thayer. I didn't know he would kill Tyrone."

His vain contact lenses caught the light as he looked at me.

# THE FALLING MAN 175

"I followed you to the motel to tell you the truth. I was going to end it, stop Norman. Then we found Tyrone, and I knew Norman had killed him. I was part of it! I couldn't tell you. I invented all that about Stanniger to say something. Then, tonight, Norman came for the money. I'd finally gotten it all. He told me about you, Shaw. All at once I couldn't go on. I couldn't let him kill twice more. I followed him to the cabin, and I shot him. I knew I'd done right at last. I had to save the girl and you."

"Noble," I said, "but not true. You were coming to kill us when the police scared you away. If you'd intended to free us, you'd have waited for the police."

"I was afraid. I was coming to help you, but when the police came you were safe, and maybe I had a chance to save myself. Norman deserved to die!"

"No," I said. "I don't think you can make even yourself believe it, but maybe you could in time. You can make yourself believe a lot. You're no killer, but you let Norman talk you into murdering Miranda, into going along with it all. You wanted to believe you couldn't stop it. If you did come to the motel to tell me, that was only a moment of fear. You didn't kill Norman to save anyone except yourself. You were afraid that he'd kill you, too. You came to the cabin to hide everything, if you could. You started with a minor theft to cheat your own company, and it led you straight to murder. And do you know what the joker is? The irony?"

He swayed in that light chair, and the rifle moved in his hands. He had little to lose by shooting McCann and me, but he had nothing to gain, either. I wasn't afraid. He had to know that McCann had men all around the house.

"The joker," I said, "is that Miranda doesn't even remember seeing Jon and you that day. She doesn't know you. She never thought about it. If you hadn't panicked, made Jon desperate, and hired Sam Norman, you had nothing to worry about."

He didn't snarl, or groan, or rage. He simply raised the rifle—left hand on the barrel, right thumb on the trigger.

I dove for him.

He had the muzzle to his right temple when I sprawled over the desk and sent the rifle flying across the room with all the strength I had in one wild swing.

McCann grabbed him. The room filled with troopers.

# 45

PERHAPS I SHOULD have let him die there in his fine, antique study.

There is no pleasure, in the end, to watching the degradation of another man, no matter what he has done. No man, if he is human, can enjoy the humiliation of another. At least, I can't. Not even a Hitler, a Beria, a Himmler—not really. That he is brought down, defeated, removed as a danger, yes, but there is no joy in watching a man on his knees crawling in the slime, tormented.

It was a long night. When we took MacDougall to the police station, Maureen was there. They'd notified her when I turned up missing, and she'd flown over from New Haven.

"Are you all right, Paul?"

"Bruised and shaky, but all right," I said. "How's the play?"

"Good. I'm getting the part. Is your case over?"

"Just about," I said.

I sent her back to my motel to get some sleep, while we worked on MacDougall. Miranda finally remembered what she had seen—under careful legal questioning before witnesses. The bullet from Norman's gun was in MacDougall's side. The rifle we took from MacDougall was the gun that had killed Norman. The tire tracks of the Lincoln were found on the back road. My statement was taken, and they got to work on the details of how MacDougall had gathered the ransom money.

MacDougall never spoke unless asked a direct question. His wound had been tended to, and if it gave him pain he said nothing. Erect and dignified, he was pushed, pulled and herded through the long night. His bear-like figure grew shaggier as the night dragged on, his head sank, his walk turned into a slow shamble. No one came from Regent-Crown, his family wasn't there, and not one friend of all those he had aided and worked for his long years in high places. When it was over he vanished into the recesses of the jail like some great white stallion being dragged through the mud, broken and forever lost.

Outside McCann's office snow flurries swirled in a gray morning sky. McCann chewed a pencil.

"We've got it all, but the prosecutor isn't going to like it. Miranda didn't actually see the film change hands. The money suggests he was involved with Norman in the kidnapping, but a good lawyer can make a case for the payoff being simple extortion; even that MacDougall was paying to save the girl."

"Norman is dead," I said, "and my statement is guesses."

"Hearsay and your judgment," McCann agreed. "I don't know how much is going to be admissible, if any of it. Norman and Calvin are both dead. They may rule out the whole theft, and everything about Thayer and Tyrone."

"You've got him for Norman." I was tired, and battered, and I hadn't eaten or really slept for a long time. And Maureen was waiting back at the motel.

"No one's going to want Norman in the headlines," McCann said. "A cop turned kidnapper and killer is bad news. And Regent-Crown'll want it all played down. A good lawyer might even try for self-defense, and MacDougall has the money for the best lawyer. He's beaten down now, but he'll revive. With what we have self-defense would be chancy, but murder-one will be just as chancy. No, we'll settle for a quiet guilty plea on manslaughter, you'll see. MacDougall's an old man. A jolt of five-to-ten, and close the books."

I got up. Snow usually makes me feel good. Today it was depressing. "Everyone'll know what he did, soon. He failed his job, he got Jon Calvin killed, he let Norman drag him down all the way. He'll lose all that matters to him, and he'll go to jail as well. His whole life comes out zero, McCann. He's a shell. He won't live five years."

I left him still chewing on the pencil, and watching the flurries of snow swirl beyond his windows. It was warm in his office, but he looked like a man who would never stop being cold again.

I went out to my car. It was battered, but it ran. I lighted a cigarette, and sat for a time with the snow falling outside, and the motor running to let the heater warm up. I did not want to go to the motel yet. She would still be asleep. If she wasn't asleep, I still wasn't ready to go to her. The case wouldn't close in my mind. I couldn't, somehow, lay it to rest yet; file it and forget it. It moved inside me, jagged and incomplete. Nothing would come to rest, settle into an answer. I felt like a man hanging above an abyss.

I drove to the hospital. Thayer was awake, but under heavy sedation.

"Taken like a kid. Me!" Thayer said.

I told him the whole story. He didn't care about most of it, not yet. Just what was important to John Thayer.

"Send the bills. You're slack on paperwork, Paul."

"I'll send them, John," I said.

"Careless. Like a stupid amateur!"

"Take it easy," I said.

"Two weeks, no longer. See that McAdams pays us. Keep on top of the Donahue girl."

"Take your time and get well," I said.

"Careless," Thayer said. "Slow, too slow."

I drove up to tell the Calvins the story. Eric Calvin opened the door, and his eyes told me that he'd heard already. His work-stained hands twisted like things apart, and his face showed confusion, mystification. To lose a son is one kind of pain, to lose a god is a different kind of pain.

He led me down to the big, homemade room with its view of the yard and the small swamp. Mrs. Calvin was there. She watched the swamp and perhaps the whole world beyond.

"I can't pay you now," Eric Calvin said. "A little at a time, okay?"

"Never mind, Mr. Calvin."

Mrs. Calvin said, "We pay our debts. Eric hired you."

"MacDougall's advance takes care of it."

Mrs. Calvin sat down. MacDougall's name had hit her. Eric Calvin went to his window—the big window in the room he had built. The snow had turned wet, it was too early in the year. Big, wet flakes melted into the swamp.

"What made him do it, Mr. Shaw?" Eric Calvin said.

"Who?" I said.

His back winced as if I had slapped him. "All of them, I guess. Funny, I never knew Norman well, but I guess I understand him best. A tough man, and there was big money.

All his life he takes risks and gets paid peanuts. Him I understand."

"No," I said, "the money was only part of it, the smallest part. The chance came, stared him in the face—a chance to humble one of the fat, squeeze a weak king, dominate the flabby. He had to take the chance to prove he was the man he had to be."

"Yeh," Calvin said, not listening at all. "Jon?"

"MacDougall offered him a big job. He wanted it."

"I never told him it should be easy! I never said there was any way except work, talent, education. I taught him to believe in what we got, yes—to want it, not to steal it."

"He believed in the result," I said. "He didn't want the work, just the reward. It happens that way sometimes."

"No moral backbone? Is that my fault?"

"You never stole. Call it our system and a flaw in Jon. Every system has its weak points, and Jon's flaw matched a weak point. Success for its own sake, without integrity."

He turned back to his window. The view was no comfort. He crossed the room, paced, sat down. "I'm asking, but I know, don't I? I just got to hear someone say it. MacDougall, too. He couldn't lose his big job, get tossed out, have nothing to do made people admire him, respect him. He couldn't get old, be a nobody, like some old machine in the dump."

He twisted his hands until they were white. His eyes shrank into his head, recalled from abstract reasons he didn't care about, to his private pain. His son.

Mrs. Calvin said, "The girl, is she really pregnant?"

"Yes."

"Could it be . . . Jon's?"

"No, Mrs. Calvin."

Her sigh was a dying breath. "That would have been nice."

They didn't notice me leave, not really. Mrs. Calvin was dreaming of the grandchild she would never have. Eric Calvin was still trying to find an explanation he could live with. Everyone wants a simple world—even me.

I had one more stop to make—one more I wanted to make, and had to make. The motel was on the way. Maureen had a right to be there anyway. She was awake, and dressed, when I arrived. I couldn't tell whether she had slept or not. Her dark eyes were distant, alone, but her pale face showed nothing else.

"Ready?" she asked.

"I'm ready, baby," I said. "I'll just pack."

The wet snow had turned to rain by the time we reached the camp. On the dirt road going in we passed Ben Mills coming out in his Lincoln. Trevino was at the wheel. Mills nodded to me, nothing more. He had forgotten his bonus offer. I didn't care. That would have made John Thayer scream in fury at me. I didn't care about that, either.

I parked near the footbridge. Cassandra's green MG was parked this side of the creek.

"Ten minutes," I said to Maureen beside me. "You want to come in with me?"

"Are there pretty young girls in there?"

"Miranda Mills," I said. "Or Miranda Levine. The girl who was kidnapped. I want to see how she is."

Her dark eyes watched my face. I felt like Tom Sawyer caught carving a girl's name on a fence. I was fooling Maureen. Sure I was.

She smiled. A soft smile. "I'll wait here for you."

I got out and walked across the footbridge in the rain. Cassandra came out of Jerry Levine's house. She looked as good as ever in a dark green wool cape and a green beret. I could feel Maureen's eyes on my back. Cassandra's eyes looked past me toward the car.

"Are you all right, Paul?" Cassandra asked.

"I'll do," I said.

Jerry Levine came out of the house behind Cassandra. Miranda was not with him, and his eyes told me not to ask to see her. The brief bridge of communication was down, the wall up again around his drop-out world. Thicker now, the wall.

"How's Miranda?" I asked.

"She's all right," he said across the gulf that would always separate us no matter what I did or thought.

Cassandra said, "She's shaken, Paul. Jerry talked to her all night after they sent her home. I think he reached her."

"What did Ben Mills want?" I asked.

Levine said, "To make Daddy noises, what else?"

"No kiss and make up, Jerry?" I said.

He didn't bother to answer me. My words were no more to

him than the cold rain that dripped from his long hair. Less; the rain was real, part of the world.

"He's her father," Cassandra said. "I think she's going to have to deal closer with reality. Not love, but perhaps recognition. She's seen our bloody side, Paul, our brief time. It might not be bad for her in the end. She's harder, but she's still broken up about Jon Calvin."

"Not the others?" I said. "An old man afraid of losing all that made him feel worthwhile, alive?"

"He bought the gold," Jerry Levine said. "He had to take it when it turned to lead, like it has to. To hell with him."

His voice was colder than any rain. In a way it had all affected him more than it had Miranda. He was brighter than Miranda, more dedicated to his beliefs in a real world instead of in some beautiful dream. He was dropping a long way out. I hoped he wouldn't drop too far. We need men who give their lives to hacking at our wilderness.

Cassandra said, "Do we feel sorry for that sergeant, too? A barbarian murderer?"

The rain trickled down my neck. "A cop in Kingston described Sam Norman—a man who rode at the edge, carried a whip, was always at war. A solitary horseman, proud of his enemies."

"The Cossack ethos, the Cossack mind," Jerry Levine said. "Maybe he died happy."

It was Levine's exit line. He turned away, and the door of his homemade house closed behind him. Cassandra and I were left in the rain. She smiled at me, beautiful in the rain, and beautiful in her elemental serenity.

"You're going to New York now?" she asked.

I nodded. "When will you be home?"

"A few days. Come and see me."

"As soon as you're back."

"No, wait a few days. Think for a few days."

"What do I think about?"

"You're a detective, you decide," she said. "You are a detective, Paul. You said it. It's your work."

She stepped to me, kissed me. Somehow, we had come to know each other very well in a few days. I held her, but my arms were stiff with the knowledge of Maureen's eyes. She backed from me toward the door of Jerry Levine's house.

"You know," she said, "I wish I'd stayed with you at the motel last night."

Then she was gone inside the house. I lighted a cigarette. The rain got it wet at once. I threw it away, and walked back across the footbridge to my car. I got in and lighted another cigarette out of the rain.

Maureen said, "The older woman I should worry about?"

She had smiled her soft smile at me before I went to Cassie. The smile that had said that we were two people who knew each other and each other's needs. Now she didn't smile. Now she waited beside me, no longer telling me that she knew all about me and my needs.

"Nothing happened," I said.

"Yes, something happened," she said. "Is it over, or don't you know yet?"

I smoked and watched the rain on the windshield. "She said she wished she'd stayed with me at the motel last night."

"It's over then," she said, and she held my arm in both her hands, rested her cheek against my shoulder. "I'm sorry, and I'm glad. I need my rock."

I started the motor and drove away from the camp to the Thruway and south. The rain stopped as we passed South Nyack. A streak of blue rested at the edge of the horizon. As we crossed the Hudson I drove faster toward the city and home.

I said, "I wish I'd gone to New Haven."

I did wish I'd gone to New Haven instead of to a motel in New Park. Was that it? When I saw Maureen on a stage I was watching myself. My dreams, dead, were alive in her, and so it was okay because she was me.

She said, "I wish I'd been here with you. I hate your work, but I need it, too, because it scares me, makes me worry about you. I'm not alone inside myself when I worry about you."

Cassandra Kingsley was the woman I so often dreamed about having. The woman I wished I needed, but didn't need. My need was Maureen. That was what Cassandra had told me back there in the rain. When she said that she wished she had stayed with me in the motel, she was saying that we should have had our one night—because there would be no more nights for us. She was saying that whatever my needs were it was Maureen who fulfilled them. My need was Maureen.

"It's over," I said as we drove over the high bridge at Spuyten Duyvil. "It never happened. Just a fool man."

"A fool human being," Maureen said. "You have me, and I have you, but that's not always what we wish we had." She squeezed my arm, rested tight against me. "We're human, and we're *us;* like it or not all the time."

I felt, then, a wave of warmth—of peace. It all slipped into place and came to rest: Cassandra, Maureen, my needs, and the whole case. That was what the whole week of danger and death came down to—that we all end up doing what we have to do, what we need to do, whether we are consciously aware of our needs or not.

I turned off the West Side Highway, and drove across town on Fifty-ninth Street toward our penthouse. We all do what we must do even though we don't know why we must do it. The hang-up inside that forced an old man to cheat, a boy to grasp at a shortcut, and a solitary Cossack to prove to the world, and to himself, that he really was a man who dared even to madness.

# ABOUT THE AUTHOR

Mark Sadler is an Edgar-winner, recipient of The Lifetime Achievement Award of The Private Eye Writers Of America, Shamus nominee and Past President of PWA. His books about modern private detective Paul Shaw reveal the rough side of our smooth world, the darkness and violence under the normal day-to-day surface. Under his other name of Michael Collins, he writes the famous adventures of PI Dan Fortune, and has received many international honors. A former New Yorker, Sadler and his wife, novelist Gayle Stone, live in Santa Barbara, California.

# LAWRENCE SANDERS

## "America's Mr. Bestseller"

| | | |
|---|---|---|
| __THE TIMOTHY FILES | 0-425-10924-0 | $4.95 |
| __CAPER | 0-425-10477-X | $4.95 |
| __THE EIGHTH COMMANDMENT | 0-425-10005-7 | $4.95 |
| __THE DREAM LOVER | 0-425-09473-1 | $4.50 |
| __THE PASSION OF MOLLY T. | 0-425-10139-8 | $4.95 |
| __THE FIRST DEADLY SIN | 0-425-10427-3 | $4.95 |
| __THE MARLOW CHRONICLES | 0-425-09963-6 | $4.50 |
| __THE PLEASURES OF HELEN | 0-425-10168-1 | $4.50 |
| __THE SECOND DEADLY SIN | 0-425-10428-1 | $4.95 |
| __THE SIXTH COMMANDMENT | 0-425-10430-3 | $4.95 |
| __THE TANGENT FACTOR | 0-425-10062-6 | $4.95 |
| __THE TANGENT OBJECTIVE | 0-425-10331-5 | $4.95 |
| __THE TENTH COMMANDMENT | 0-425-10431-1 | $4.95 |
| __THE TOMORROW FILE | 0-425-08179-6 | $4.95 |
| __THE THIRD DEADLY SIN | 0-425-10429-X | $4.95 |
| __THE ANDERSON TAPES | 0-425-10364-1 | $4.95 |
| __THE CASE OF LUCY BENDING | 0-425-10086-3 | $4.50 |
| __THE SEDUCTION OF PETER S. | 0-425-09314-X | $4.95 |
| __THE LOVES OF HARRY DANCER | 0-425-08473-6 | $4.50 |
| __THE FOURTH DEADLY SIN | 0-425-09078-7 | $4.95 |

Please send the titles I've checked above. Mail orders to:

**BERKLEY PUBLISHING GROUP**
390 Murray Hill Pkwy., Dept. B
East Rutherford, NJ 07073

NAME _____
ADDRESS _____
CITY _____
STATE _____ ZIP _____

Please allow 6 weeks for delivery.
Prices are subject to change without notice.

POSTAGE & HANDLING:
$1.00 for one book, $.25 for each additional. Do not exceed $3.50.

| | |
|---|---|
| BOOK TOTAL | $_____ |
| SHIPPING & HANDLING | $_____ |
| APPLICABLE SALES TAX (CA, NJ, NY, PA) | $_____ |
| TOTAL AMOUNT DUE | $_____ |

PAYABLE IN US FUNDS.
(No cash orders accepted.)

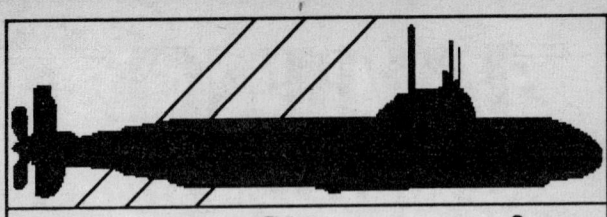

# Tom Clancy's

## #1 NEW YORK TIMES BESTSELLERS

__ **THE HUNT FOR RED OCTOBER**    0-425-08383-7/$4.95
"The Perfect Yarn."—President Ronald Reagan
"A fine thriller...flawless authenticity, frighteningly genuine."—*The Wall Street Journal*

__ **RED STORM RISING**    0-425-10107-X/$4.95
"Brilliant...staccato suspense."—*Newsweek*
"Exciting...fast and furious."—*USA Today*

__ **PATRIOT GAMES**    0-425-10972-0/$4.95
"Elegant...A novel that crackles."—*New York Times*
"Marvelously tense...He is a master of the genre he seems to have created."—*Publishers Weekly*

**THE CARDINAL OF THE KREMLIN**
(On sale August 1989)
"The best of the Jack Ryan series!"—*New York Times*
"Fast and fascinating!"—*Chicago Tribune*

---

Check book(s). Fill out coupon. Send to:

BERKLEY PUBLISHING GROUP
390 Murray Hill Pkwy., Dept. B
East Rutherford, NJ 07073

NAME_____
ADDRESS_____
CITY_____
STATE_____ZIP_____

PLEASE ALLOW 6 WEEKS FOR DELIVERY.
PRICES ARE SUBJECT TO CHANGE
WITHOUT NOTICE.

POSTAGE AND HANDLING:
$1.00 for one book, 25¢ for each additional. Do not exceed $3.50.

BOOK TOTAL    $_____
POSTAGE & HANDLING    $_____
APPLICABLE SALES TAX    $_____
(CA, NJ, NY, PA)
TOTAL AMOUNT DUE    $_____
PAYABLE IN US FUNDS.
(No cash orders accepted.)

190